SMARTER
BARTER

SMARTER BARTER

A Guide for Corporations,
Professionals and Small Businesses

Michael Gershman

VIKING

VIKING
Viking Penguin Inc., 40 West 23rd Street,
New York, New York 10010, U.S.A.
Penguin Books Ltd, Harmondsworth,
Middlesex, England
Penguin Books Australia Ltd, Ringwood,
Victoria, Australia
Penguin Books Canada Limited, 2801 John Street,
Markham, Ontario, Canada L3R 1B4
Penguin Books (N.Z.) Ltd, 182–190 Wairau Road,
Auckland 10, New Zealand

First published in 1986 by Viking Penguin Inc.
Published simultaneously in Canada

LIBRARY OF CONGRESS CATALOGING IN PUBLICATION DATA
Gershman, Michael.
    Smarter barter.
    Bibliography: p.
    1. Barter.   I. Title.
HF1019.G47   1986   658.8′4   86-5602
ISBN 0-670-81273-0

Printed in the United States of America by
The Book Press, Brattleboro, Vermont
Design by Robert Bull
Set in Bodoni Book

To SKG, my favorite best-selling author.

ACKNOWLEDGMENTS

The world of business barter is a unique demimonde. I could not have learned what I know about it without the cooperation of many people who were willing to talk about it on the record, some of them for the first time.

I would be remiss in not mentioning the special contributions made by the following people in the writing of this book:

Bill Nordstrom, who got me into the barter business; Bob Twersky for his hands-on knowledge of barter in the marketplace; Bill Hokanson for his expertise in corporate bartering; Bob Meyer for numerous leads and information; Fred Howell, who helped lead me through the maze of countertrade; my agent Kathy Robbins. I owe special thanks to my editor, Gerry Howard, for his patience, acute analysis and numerous organizational suggestions.

I would also like to thank the following organizations for their cooperation in the preparation of this manuscript: Avis Corp.; Barter Exchange; Broadcast Marketing; Business Exchange; Corporate Trade Center; *Countertrade & Barter Quarterly;* Countertrade Roundtable; Integrated Barter International; K mart Trading Services; Korn/Ferry International; Lockheed; 3M Corp.; McDonnell Douglas; Media General Broadcast Services; Northrop Aviation; Philadelphia First Group; Republic Airlines; Sears World Trade; J. Walter Thompson; U.S. Dept. of Commerce; U.S. Dept. of the Treasury; U.S. Internal Revenue Service; U.S. Steel; Universal Trade Exchange.

Finally, the following individuals provided leads, information and assistance of various kinds: Lee Albert, Dick Auletta, Mike

Carruthers, Rocky Chatham, Roger Davis, Linda Dickerson, Bill Francisco, Sherry Gear, Robb Giannangeli, Alicia Johnson, A. D. Kessler, Art Kramer, Nino Lucio, Bob Morgan, Frank Vuono and Dave Wagenvoord.

CONTENTS

INTRODUCTION

What sort of man reads *Cosmopolitan*? Someone on an airplane who can't find a copy of *Sports Illustrated, Newsweek, GQ, Forbes, Harper's, Grit* or *Progressive Grocer*, that's who.

Yet, tucked in between "Thin Thighs in Thirty Seconds" and "Favorite Positions of Hollywood Physicians," I found an excerpt from a book about barter. I read what Dyanne Asimow Simon had to say about the subject and was intrigued. In her view, barter is "guerrilla economics" because it "eliminates corporate overhead, gets rid of middlemen and punctures the abstract and illusory power of money."

I subsequently read Simon's entire book; while a portion of it is devoted to barter as a business tool, *The Barter Book* focuses mainly on adapting rural swapping to urban survival and using barter as a socioeconomic tool to bind neighborhoods and communities closer together. I later read several other books (*Back to Barter, How to Barter and Swap*) which also concentrate on barter's place in the back-to-the-land movement of the 1960s and thought I had exhausted the subject.

I was wrong.

In 1981, a whole chain of circumstances led me to join and also publicize a trade exchange—a local business which brokers its members' goods and services on a barter basis. Since then, I've read everything I could put my hands on about barter, have questioned hundreds of business people about their experiences with it, have lectured and taken part in seminars about it.

I have even learned, unbeknownst to me, that Jack Lobell, my late grandfather, bartered.

In the excellent *Let's Try Barter,* Charles Morrow Wilson writes, "Jack Lobell, a professional supplier to garment-making firms, has established the Ocean Pearl Button Service as a gratis service. . . . He invites clients and others to submit samples of buttons which they have on hand and do not currently need, and distributes the samples to garment makers. . . . In this way manufacturers are enabled to barter their unused stocks for needed ones or to utilize inventories which would otherwise be obsolete and worthless."

This unexpected personal connection typifies the reason that barter hasn't lost its fascination for me. As in the above example, there's something supremely logical about barter, and, while it can be applied in a variety of complex situations, it remains a simple technique.

Unfortunately, that very simplicity has led some executives mistakenly to equate barter with primitive methods and has made them think there's nothing more they need to learn about it. Since sophisticated corporations like U.S. Steel, General Motors, 3M, CBS-TV, and Northrop have bartered successfully as has nearly every other *Fortune* 500 corporation, such an outworn attitude needs drastic updating. Corporations such as these repeatedly use barter to open new markets, increase cash flow, reduce fixed overhead, create new channels of distribution, and achieve a variety of other business objectives.

Because barter is a business tool that doesn't use money, some people have had problems understanding it; however, when a technique applicable to marketing, finance and purchasing can help professionals increase their billable time, manufacturers decrease their excess production capacity and allow entire industries like broadcasting and travel to lessen the effects of seasonal slowdowns, it deserves as much study as management, sales promotion or any other business field sorely in need of excellence.

Since picking up that issue of *Cosmopolitan,* I've observed the beneficial effects of bartering on the economics of various professionals and a variety of businesses of all sizes. I've seen it turn liabilities into assets, give its users compelling marketing advantages and conserve corporate cash in a variety of ways. While the half dozen other books on barter, like Dyanne Simon's, contain valuable information on the individual and neighborhood aspects of trading, they barely mention its numerous business applications. That's why I wrote this book.

I believe every business person needs to know what bartering can—and cannot—do, when to use it, what to use it for, and how to structure a barter deal. *Smarter Barter* begins with an overview of barter, focuses on the evolution of money, describes the basics of bartering, the IRS view of barter, and then outlines the various forms of business bartering, progressing from the simplest to the most complex. Beginning with reciprocal trade (which can be likened to swapping baseball cards), the book details the workings of trade exchanges and corporate barter brokers, outlines how media and travel are traded, discusses international barter (countertrade) on both corporate and government levels and concludes with an analysis of barter's future.

I hope a book-length treatment of barter's place in business will dispel some of the myths about it—"It's a way to cheat on your taxes," "It's a scam," "It's illegal." When a reporter interviewing me mentioned that his search of the Lexis data base resulted in nearly four hundred articles on the subject, I wondered how many had been read and digested because, clearly, all this media attention hasn't necessarily translated into comprehension.

For one thing, many people still don't understand barter for what it is—a neutral business tool, neither positive nor negative. Some people remain suspicious of it, which is as rational as hating postage meters or any other business tool. Secondly, just as there are creative ways to multiply cash as in the leveraged buy-outs which have become so familiar to business page readers, there are *more* ways to do exactly the same thing by trading goods and services. (See Chapter 7.)

Finally, as useful as barter is, there are probably ways to use it that haven't been fully explored yet, or will change as business technology changes. While barter won't do much for your waistline, as some of its wilder proponents have claimed, it can do wonders for your bottom line. For that reason, you owe it to yourself and your company to become smarter about barter.

MICHAEL GERSHMAN
Los Angeles, California
February 1986

CHAPTER 1

THE $600 BILLION
MISUNDERSTANDING

---

*"If I had my life to live all over again, I would elect to
be a trader of goods rather than a student of sciences. . . .
I think barter is a noble thing. I need to know much more
about it."*
—ALBERT EINSTEIN, as quoted in *Let's Try Barter*

Einstein made this comment after a tour of Navajo trading posts
in the mid-1930s had impressed him with barter's economic utility. Were he alive today, he'd be pleased to know that, in the intervening fifty years, his "noble thing" has expanded nearly as
quickly as the universe. Countertrade, international bartering,
has blossomed to the point where it alone amounts to an annual
$600 billion business—one fourth of all world trade—according
to the U.S. Department of Commerce.

Throw in media, hotel and travel trading, deals made through
trade exchanges and barter brokerages, reciprocal trades, mortgage swaps and real estate exchanges, and bartering becomes
more than a trillion-dollar proposition on a global basis.

Yet sheer volume hasn't led to complete acceptance or understanding of trading for several reasons. For one thing, some
people barter without even realizing it; others barter without ad-
mitting it. I met the assistant publisher of *California* magazine
over dinner at a Beverly Hills restaurant. After discovering that I
was writing a book about barter, he groaned about the practice;
"It costs me money; once an advertiser has gone into our maga-

1

zine on a barter basis, he'll never pay cash." At the end of his five-minute harangue, he blithely signed the check and smiled at me. He explained, "We have a 'trade-out deal' with the restaurant."

California's management had obviously made an arrangement to trade advertising space for meals at the restaurant; I, too, have traded for meals as well as carpeting for my home and long-distance telephone, printing and messenger service for the publicity business I owned before I began writing books. I got started in barter by becoming a member of and publicist for a Los Angeles trade exchange (a local barter brokerage) and ended up by editing *On Trade*, a barter magazine that circulated in twelve cities.

On Trade gave me access to executives at Xerox Corp., Continental Airlines, Amfac Hotels and Twentieth Century–Fox, amusement park owners in Utah, bankers in California, teleconferencing-equipment supplies in Oregon and horse syndicators in Georgia. I interviewed an industrial economist who moonlighted by handicapping football games, a woman who made her living by swapping other people's vacation homes, and a group of entrepreneurs that ran the gamut from restaurant franchisees and executive search firms to broadcasters and real estate developers.

I learned that while nearly everybody barters, nearly nobody wants to use the dreaded word. People in the restaurant business refer to "trade-outs," "scrip" and "special discount coupons." Ask a real estate agent if he or she barters, and you'll get a cold stare. Instead, ask if he or she is an "exchangor," the approved industry term for people who exchange real estate, and you'll get a ten-minute sermon on why it has become a $25 billion business.

Hotel owners don't barter, of course, but they will admit to issuing "limited availability use certificates." In the same vein, broadcasters don't barter either, but they do accept "merchandise for promotional considerations" in exchange for air time. Airlines never ever barter; they just issue "exchange vouchers" to travel agents or advertising agents. Finally, aerospace companies never export airplanes on a barter basis; however, they will accept "offset considerations" like computer paper, air travel and canned ham. This flurry of nonactivity leads me to conclude that, if bartering is a $600 billion business, not-bartering must be at least twice as big.

As ludicrous as the special jargon and the secrecy can be, they're really minor factors in the widespread misunderstanding of what barter really is and what it can do for a business. Barter is simply a technique for the direct exchange of commodities without the use of money or some other medium of exchange. The *Encyclopaedia Britannica* says in its entry on barter, "However the processes of exchange may be disguised by the immediate translation of goods into money or money into goods, all trade essentially remains barter."

Why, then, do business people devote so much passion, time and energy to keep their bartering a secret?

There are basically four reasons. First, barter has always labored under the connotation of being mainly a method to unload distressed or unsalable merchandise, when it actually has numerous other uses. Second, many people simply can't understand how a noncash transaction works due to prior conditioning and lack of imagination. Third, not declaring income obtained through barter used to be a favorite illicit way to keep the tax bill down until Congress passed the 1982 Tax Equity and Fiscal Responsibility Act. Finally, barter has received negative publicity due to the quick birth, boom and bust of some franchised trade exchanges. (See Chapter 6.)

Yet the bad publicity and the negative connotations haven't slowed its growth. If anything, barter is bigger than ever, because it makes so much sense economically. Sears, McDonnell Douglas, 3M and General Motors long ago set up their own trading companies to handle such activities; B. F. Goodrich swapped more than $1 million worth of tires for a company jet, and PepsiCo trades $30 million worth of goods annually, according to the *Connecticut Business Journal.*

Why do huge companies barter?

- **It increases cash flow.** Xerox bartered $1.7 million worth of computers, typewriters, and used computers to pay for two years of a five-year office lease and was able to spend on other things the dollars it saved.

- **It reduces excess inventory.** Saddled with twenty-five planes it couldn't sell for the cash price it wanted, McDonnell Douglas Corp. traded them for electronic parts, heavy machinery and a variety of other items from Yugoslavia.
- **It attracts new customers inexpensively.** Through a corporate barter broker, U.S. Steel was able to increase production of specialized steel products and to find new customers for them by bartering.

While it's true that giant corporations trade, bartering is not just for the corporate upper crust; the equation works the same whether the commodity being traded is unused production time (as above), jet aircraft, excess time (as in broadcast advertising), dental or accounting services, unused space (as in an empty hotel room or airline seat), videocassettes or tires. That's why small businesses and professionals trade with each other one-on-one or do their bartering in larger amounts through trade exchanges.

A trade exchange brings buyer and seller together using barter dollars rather than cash dollars as a medium of exchange. Hundreds of lawyers, tire dealers, physicians, jewelers, and PR firms use this method to locate new customers, conserve cash and eliminate unwanted inventory. After members sign up, their wares—services, goods, whatever—are offered for trade on a commission basis. When a buyer is interested in making a purchase, the exchange authorizes it like an American Express or MasterCard purchase, credits the seller, debits the buyer and records the transaction for the IRS in trade dollars.

Of course, people have bartered for five thousand years without trade exchanges as four art-related examples show. Pablo Picasso bartered paintings for art supplies; Henry Miller swapped his watercolors for the services of a heart specialist; artist Joan Miro's widow settled an outstanding tax bill with some of his paintings. Finally, when no West German bank would allow Warren Beatty to film a scene for the movie *$$$*, a museum let him

build a set in an unused wing; in return, Beatty bought and donated two paintings to the museum.

The chances are good that, at some time in your life, you too
have swapped your own expertise for advice on your taxes, your
carburetor or your sciatica, baked cookies to thank someone
for house-sitting or swapped your slightly broken rocking chair
for a landscape lying in someone's attic. Just as Molière's *bour-
geois gentilhomme* was surprised to learn he'd been speaking
prose all his life, you may have been bartering for years without
realizing it.

Thomas Edison realized barter's usefulness in 1922 when he
proposed a commodity-based currency, and bartering became
widespread in the early and mid-1930s as work and purchasing
power dried up. The Depression made bartering an economic necessity, and thousands of people joined local "trade clubs" and
"work exchanges," the precursors of trade exchanges. By the
end of the 1930s, Adolf Hitler, cut off from normal trade relations with other nations, was using barter to build his war machine.

After World War II ended, cigarettes became the favored
medium of exchange throughout Europe in the wake of a shortage of hard currency. When ideology prevented hard currency
from leaving East bloc countries in the late 1940s, countertrade
began to boom between East and West. Most recently, the "oil
crisis" of the 1970s forced countries to buy petroleum products
with other commodities when they ran short of cash, and the
South American credit crunch also fueled bartering as countries
like Brazil traded agricultural products for needed machinery.

Despite this activity, barter has been regarded in the United
States, until recently, strictly as a method manufacturers used to
dump shelf-clogging merchandise, but all that is changing. Now,
virtually every major corporation has executives responsible for
seeing that excess inventory or capacity is bartered. What made
giant companies, small businesses and professionals suddenly
take notice of barter in the 1970s? In short, economics made it
necessary, credits made it possible, computers made it fast, and
acceptance made it respectable.

THE CURRENCY SHORTAGE

Money—the commodity originally invented to make trading easier—is now often an impediment to commerce because cash is in
such short supply. Given this condition, barter's inherent flexibility as a medium of exchange—allowing a wide variety of goods
and services to take the place of cash—made it look a lot more
promising. Robert Mamis wrote in an article in *Inc.* magazine, "A
small rose in a vast onion patch, the concept of barter clearly
smells sweet to [a world] burdened by inflation, recession, shortages of cash, tight credit, slumping sales, surplus inventory, and
the host of other ills that business is heir to."

Barter first began making a serious comeback during the
1973–74 recession. Corporate giants that had bartered tradition-
ally—oil and chemical companies, radio and TV stations, airlines
and hotels—stepped up their activities, while other corporations
seriously began to investigate barter for the first time. A 1973
survey done by *Purchasing World* made waves in the corporate
world by reporting that 48 percent of U.S. companies large
enough to employ purchasing agents were already bartering.

Confirmed barterer Karl Hess, formerly a speech writer for
Senator Barry Goldwater, says,"Paper money circulates throughout the world and is still the major medium of exchange. But more
and more, commodities, from gold to oil to wheat to land, are becoming the real 'hard' currencies, everywhere rising in value
while the value of paper monies just about everywhere drops and
drops." A Kuwaiti oil minister told Adam Smith, "Our oil is worth
more in the ground than your paper money." Yet, when the oil
"crisis" was eventually transformed into a "glut," OPEC countries busily bartered their black gold for jet planes, heavy machinery and computer technology.

MAKING TRADING EASIER

Before computers, satellites and telecommunications became
facts of business life, even people who *wanted* to barter had difficulty arranging trades. Barter was common among farmers, but,

in the business world, it was an afterthought, a proposition purely of the moment—face-to-face, here-and-now, take-it-or-leave-it. Then, in the late 1950s, barter pioneer and former banker Marvin "Mac" McConnell came up with a way to simplify things. At first envisioning what he calls "a big pool of shared due bills," he applied his banking background to create the trade credit (or trade dollar) and promoted the benefits of *indirect trading*.

He reasoned that allowing his customers to trade their goods and services for credits—which could then be used at a later date—was far more efficient than their trying to swap products and services directly and immediately in a reciprocal, or one-on-one, trade. Using credits, the need for each party to find a trading partner (and simultaneously negotiate the details) was magically eliminated. The upshot was that plumbers no longer needed to find tire dealers to trade with directly; Business Exchange, McConnell's company, did it for them and charged a commission for its services.

McConnell's brainstorm provided a low-risk way for professionals and small businesses to increase their customer base and, in the process, made a new generic business called the trade exchange workable. As a sensational by-product, it also made intercity bartering possible. A Los Angeles lawyer could now trade with a Denver motel, because each was using a common currency called a trade dollar. Thus, McConnell's insight changed what was, at best, a clumsy business into a streamlined market for buyers and sellers. While the trade exchange was initially intended for small retail businesses, it also made national trading possible, inevitably getting major corporations more interested in barter as well.

THE RISE OF THE COMPUTER

When the computer became a fact of business life, barter gained immediacy as a way of doing business. Trend-spotter Alvin Toffler had already predicted the phenomenon in *The Third Wave:* "Money supplanted barter in the past partly because it was so difficult to keep track of complex swaps involving many different kinds of measurement. . . . The growing availability of computers, however, makes it easier to record extremely complex trades and therefore makes money, as such, less essential."

By now, most of us are familiar with the computer's facility with projections, spreadsheets, word processing, mailing list maintenance, etc. Mated with a barter-based economic system, the computer can:

- **match buyers and sellers.** All national barter companies and nearly all local trade exchanges now maintain "want" lists and "have" lists which can be searched and matched by computer on a daily, if not hourly, basis. In this way, a prospective member or client can find out whether a specific item is available even before he or she signs up.
- **provide credit checks and authorizations.** Just as Master-Card and Visa transactions can be authorized by computer, similar cards issued by trade exchanges can be used to verify account balances and provide authorizations.
- **perform accounting functions.** Computers have made running a barter business a lot simpler and much easier to account for by assigning credits and debits, noting a given transaction's effect on inventory, supply and demand, and printing statements automatically.

With computers in place almost everywhere, barter deals can be completed with the finality of cash and even greater speed. *Business Week* says, "Developments in telecommunications [have] made it as easy to transfer funds from Bahrain to Zurich as from Boston to Palm Beach." When Continental Airlines traded $1.4 million worth of airline tickets for hotel rooms to put up its flight crews, the trade dollars it earned were credited and became spendable instantaneously; there was no waiting period so the check could clear.

Computers are even making Uncle Sam more amenable to barter. Trademark Barter Banking, Portland, Oregon, processes one thousand transactions a week for each of its twenty-five affiliated trade exchanges. With approval from the U.S. Internal Revenue Service, Trademark printed 1.5 million copies of its own Form 1099-B and sent them to Washington in compliance with the transactional reporting requirements the IRS eventually adopted in 1983 following passage of the 1982 tax bill. Also, by posting a $2.5 million bond with the Federal Reserve System, Trademark has been allowed to debit clients' cash accounts for transaction fees electronically.

Similarly, International Business Clearinghouse (IBC) is a service offered to the world's 1.5 million telex customers through Western Union. Owned by Barter Worldwide, Inc., Los Angeles, IBC offers an electronic bulletin board for buyers and sellers of goods—both cash and barter—and also puts buyers and sellers together for a commission ranging from 5 to 10 percent.

Despite these technological changes, we are still instructed to think that cash is somehow more "real" than other commodities because of its liquidity. Moreton Binn, president of Atwood Richards, which annually arranges trades in nine figures, disagrees. He says, "Money buys you a bit of time and convenience, that's all. . . . You don't eat the dollar. You don't wear it. It's really only a bartering tool."

INCREASING RESPECTABILITY

During the mid-1970s the energy crisis, a cash and credit crunch and the computer gave barter a big boost; however, naysayers could still sniff, "Oh sure, it's great if you want to cheat on your taxes," or "What if they go out of business?" Numerous trade exchanges *did* come into and go out of business with the speed of summer lightning; many barterers *didn't* report their trade income.

Amid much fanfare, the IRS announced Project Barter, an investigation of 2,600 barterers' returns; it eventually netted the government an additional $700,000 in taxes. But the same survey showed *non-barterers'* returns averaged additional taxes and penalties of $1,563, while auditing barterers' returns turned up an average of only $556 in additional taxes and penalties. More-over, the computer, company-issued credit cards and three-part forms like those used by American Express, MasterCard and Visa have made audit trails a fact of life for trade exchanges and have made cheating riskier business for would-be tax evaders.

More importantly, the local trade exchange is evolving into a more corporate entity with greater fiscal controls. Three new public barter companies—Univex, Integrated Barter and Barter Exchange—feature board members like former Citicorp President William I. Spencer, former Schroder's Bank CEO Mark Maged and Everett Keech, assistant dean of the Wharton School of Business.

This infusion of boardroom gray follows hot on the heels of barter's single biggest boost toward respectability. The 1982 tax bill amended the Internal Revenue Code and gave trade ex-changes "third-party record-keeper status," the same legal standing as that enjoyed by banks, securities brokerages and credit-card companies. Finally, the International Reciprocal Trade Association (IRTA), the trade association for trade ex-changes, has helped introduce a bill into Congress requiring the licensing of trade exchanges under the auspices of the Depart-ment of Commerce.

Barter has become so respectable that even Uncle Sam trades. Public Law 96–41, enacted in 1979, says, "The President shall encourage the use of barter in the acquisition of strategic materials." The law was passed to reinstate the kind of swapping that the government did from 1950 to 1967 when $12 billion worth of strategic materials was obtained from fifty different countries according to the Department of Agriculture; it was dis-continued in 1973 due to pressure from the Canadian-American grain lobby, according to author Dyanne Asimow Simon in *The Barter Book.*

Falling export sales caused an about-face, and, in 1982, Uncle Sam swapped $13 million worth of dairy products for 400,000 tons of Jamaican bauxite. In addition, the Senate Agricultural Committee has passed legislation enabling the government to barter surplus stocks of the Commodity Credit Corporation for petroleum products when U.S. reserves fall below legal limits.

All of these factors—decreased cash and transaction time and increased convenience and respectability—have given Einstein's comment about barter an air of prophecy and have made it a business alternative worth exploring. With governments, corporations, small businesses and professionals doing more and more business without money, you need to know the who, what, when, where, why and how of bartering. The best way to begin is by learning how commerce was carried on B.C.—before cash.

CHAPTER 2

BARTER, MONEY
AND COMMERCE

Money does not pay for anything, never has, never will. It is an economic axiom as old as the hills that goods and services can be paid for only with goods and services.
—ALBERT JAY NOCK, *Memoirs of a Superfluous Man*

Despite Nock's insight, early training at home and in school has made us think of only two very specific things as real money—paper dollars and metal coins. We can't imagine money as being anything else, and, conversely, we can't imagine anything else as being money.

This very limited view of what money can be is one of the main reasons that business people misunderstand barter. I've heard seasoned executives say things like "I *know* what you're talking about, but I just can't *see* it." Or "Yes, I understand perfectly; now tell me, how does it *really* work?" Psychotherapist Dr. Karen Dean Fritts, a regular contributor to TV's "Hour Magazine," understands the reason that underlies such reactions. She says, "Human beings are taught to invest a certain emotional power in money. Once that training takes hold, they will naturally want to devalue anything that replaces money."

Curiously, because barter transactions allow a wider range of options in the methods of payment—any forms mutually agreeable to both buyer and seller—elasticity breeds contempt. Money

13

is one of our ties to reality; if anything can be money, and money can be anything, then the world has gone mad.

In addition to money's psychological underpinning, it has religious connotations that go back centuries. Clay tablets, which served as money, were stored in Babylonian and Greek temples; many banks are clearly patterned after Roman temples; our paper money bears the legend "In God we trust." The very word "money" comes to us from the Roman temple that goddess Juno Moneta zealously guarded, because it was the place where coins were minted.

Given these three powerful forces—education, psychology and religion—it's no wonder that people have difficulty considering objects like playing cards, leather or tobacco as currency. Yet, at various times in the past, Canadian soldiers have been paid in playing cards, Frenchmen in leather, and Englishmen in flint or nails. Virginia tobacco, New Guinea boar tusks, whale teeth in Fiji, feathers in Santa Cruz, rats on Easter Island and mahogany logs in British Honduras—all have served as money.

Some of these items appear to have little utility, yet, as Adam Smith points out in *The Money Game,* "Money is useless; that is, it must literally be useless in order to be money, whether the money is the stone cartwheels of Yap island, shells, dogs' teeth, gold stored in Fort Knox, or East African cattle that can't be eaten because that would be—literally—eating up capital."

In less sophisticated times, however, money did have utility, and axes, reindeer, blankets, woodpeckers' scalps, fishhooks, rat traps and bullets have all served as currency. Court records from Massachusetts show an Indian was fined a beaver skin for shooting a colonist's pig. By 1635, the state was using musket bullets as money, and, in 1649, one enterprising Harvard student settled his bill with the payment of an old cow.

That tangible objects like these were used as forms of payment is even more interesting in light of the fact that abstract money has been around in one form or another for 4,500 years. In *Primitive Money,* professor Paul Einzig of the University of London says, "It is reasonable to assume that money was first developed to serve matrimonial, political or religious purposes and was only later developed for the purposes of general commerce. . . . Money tends to develop automatically out of barter through the fact that favorite means of barter are apt to arise. A stage is usually reached when the use of one of these means of barter becomes so widespread that it may be said to have become a medium of exchange."

Most anthropologists and historians of economics agree that barter began as an exchange of gifts and evolved quite naturally into the succeeding stage—silent barter. Silent barter, a process in which goods are literally left in a specific location for display and possible trade, marked the beginning of international commerce. The modern equivalent would involve leaving an unwanted car at a busy intersection in hopes that someone might be interested in swapping for it.

We don't have to do business that way, because we have a recognized medium of exchange—cash—and established places to exchange that cash for goods—stores. However, silent barter (or silent trade) merits close inspection, because its underlying principle is the same one which fuels modern bartering—the double coincidence of wants. (You want my raccoon coat; I want your pool cover; we trade, and everybody's happy.)

In *The Evolution of Money,* Rupert J. Ederer describes silent barter this way: "The party initiating the exchange would leave merchandise of which he wished to rid himself in a designated place . . . one which the other party could scarcely avoid noticing. . . . Should the neighbor take what was offered as a windfall and neglect to offer anything in exchange, tribal war could easily ensue. It was to avoid such consequences that retaliation in roughly equal measure probably began."

In the next stage of commerce, rather than leaving goods someplace for inspection, neither party gave anything at all until an arrangement satisfactory to both was reached. It should come as no surprise that cattle were the first prized commodity in open barter and quickly became the most traded possession in agricultural societies. They saved labor and served as sources of food, clothing (breechclouts) and shelter (the hides were used in tents or lean-tos). In *The Iliad,* Homer valued shields in terms of cattle, which are still used as currency in Africa and South America.

If numerous historians hadn't already noted cattle's use as the first medium of exchange, we could understand its preeminence by looking in the dictionary. The Latin word for "money," *pecunia,* comes from *pecus,* cattle. Likewise, "capital" is derived from the Latin word *capita* meaning a head of cattle (hence, Adam Smith's pun above). When we pay someone a "fee," we are using the German word *vieh,* which refers to cattle. Similarly, the Sanskrit word *rupya* means cattle and is the source of the "rupee," India's currency. Finally, in English, the word "cattle" or its close relative, "chattel," has come to include *all* property, as in a chattel mortgage.

As we have seen, "money" can be food, animals, tools, minerals, weapons, etc. It's an economic truism that money can be anything that does the work of money. Any currency or other form of money has five functions. It must be:

- **a recognized means of exchange**—a commodity generally and freely accepted for goods and services
- **a measure of value which serves as a standard for other commodities.** Just as we express length in terms of meters and feet and weight in terms of kilograms or pounds, so we express value in terms of the dollar, franc, yen, or pound— originally a pound's weight of sterling silver.
- **a storehouse of value.** It must possess some continuing value in and of itself and have value economically—i.e., scarcity. (When money is printed in job lots, its value is deflated.) Money is currently the most marketable commodity one can possess, due to its liquidity. In times of stress, you might not be able to sell stocks, bonds, land, art or jewelry, but, generally, you can always "sell" your money for commodities, making money the most "salable" commodity.
- **a standard of deferred payments.** Suppose you sell something, deliver the goods today and don't receive your money

until some time later. Owing to your generous nature, a debt has been created, and that debt is expressed in terms of money.

■ **a unit for bank reserves.** Bank deposits and bank notes are usually payable on demand in legal tender—whatever currency the state recognizes as money. For that reason, banks must always have a certain amount of such money available to meet the demands of their depositors.

By this definition, it is easy to see how foodstuffs qualified as money. They had value and scarcity and were generally recognized as currency. In ancient Egypt, bread was used as currency, and Egyptian kings took grain for rent and taxes, making granaries, in a sense, the first banks. Grain is still used to make purchases in China, India, Mexico and the Philippines. Until the nineteenth century, British farmers paid their rents in grain, and fermented grain—beer—partially paid wages in some coal mines. (A commission investigating its efficiency as money around 1850 reported, "This currency is very popular, and highly liquid, but it is issued to excess and is difficult to store.")

As time and trade went on, other forms of money with no tangible value began to be accepted. When the Dutch town of Leyden was under attack in 1572, silver and other valuables disappeared. Citizens took books from the town library, tore out pages, glued them together and used them as currency; after the siege, the "book money" was redeemed. In 1685, bad weather delayed the delivery from England of payments due Canadian soldiers. A creative proconsul in Canada ordered all playing cards requisitioned, assigned them three different values and validated them with his signature; playing card money remained in circulation until 1749.

Today, on the Polynesian island of Yap, huge limestones—up to twelve feet in diameter—are still used as currency, and a Yap islander can still trade a thirty-inch limestone wheel for a wife; a medium wheel is equal to a canoe, and a six-foot wheel is worth a whole village. Physical possession is not necessary. (For that reason, tribesmen often make journeys to see their money into family outings.)

Being more sophisticated, colonial settlers used seashells—wampum—as the first currency in the New World. In the beginning, Indians would not readily accept metal coins in trade, and English settlers were obliged to polish and string white, blue or black beads made from clam, mussel and oyster shells into belts or sashes. Three black beads or four white ones were worth a penny, and in 1641 wampum was made legal tender for debts up to ten pounds in Massachusetts. Naturally, some individuals began counterfeiting wampum, and one entrepreneur set up a factory to turn white beads black; wampum rapidly became worthless, and eventually tobacco became America's prime currency.

Custom became law in 1642 when Virginia passed an act forbidding the making of contracts payable in money and making tobacco the sole currency. Naturally, people started planting tobacco and by 1665, it sold for only a penny a pound. Huge quantities were then burned at government request to jack up the price. Colonists had begun minting their own money in 1652, and firms like the Hudson Bay Company issued beaver-shaped tokens valued at one beaver skin apiece, although Great Britain tried to prevent the practice. In 1751, Parliament banned the New England colonies from issuing paper money, and, on April 19, 1764, the practice was also banned in Virginia, uniting the commercial colonies in the North with the agricultural colonies in the South against Britain's policies and making war inevitable.

Two months after Paul Revere's ride, the Second Continental Congress voted to issue $2 million in bills of credit to support the army. When the colonists finally broke with the mother country and formed the Continental Army, paper money was printed . . . and printed, giving rise to the expression, "not worth a Continental." On March 18, 1780, Congress passed the Forty to One Act, which provided that Continental paper money be redeemed at one fortieth its face value, just as Germany's mark would be devalued in 1923.

The states reverted to printing money again in the midst of a postwar depression in 1786, and, on August 5, 1786, Congress adopted a system of coinage; the first coin bearing the name of the United States of America was the Fugio cent of 1787, designed by Benjamin Franklin, which carried the pithy motto, MIND YOUR BUSINESS. Only American coins and bills have served as currency since, with one exception. On July 17, 1862, Congress authorized the printing of "postage currency," stamps which could be used as legal tender and which remained in circulation until 1876.

Ever since then, American paper money and coinage has evolved and has become accepted internationally. Just as the British pound was accepted worldwide in the nineteenth century, American money is now the benchmark in international finance, although, as noted, the American cigarette proved to be as popular if less official for a brief while in postwar Europe. (In fact, economic historian Einzig even suggested that American cigarettes be established up as the official money for Europe after World War II.) In October 1945, *Newsweek* reported that in Vienna twelve packs would buy a Leica camera, while in Rome, ten packs bought one night of a prostitute's time.

Whether or not the idea arose from Einzig's proposal, the first of several Overseas Barter Centers was established by the U.S. occupational forces in Frankfurt, Germany, in May 1948. These Centers allowed German citizens to barter their belongings with U.S. soldiers, using American cigarettes and other goods. Barterers entered an appraising office, and German citizens working with the U.S. armed forces evaluated the offerings and gave donors printed slips of paper which stated the number of barter points earned through exchanging; daily quotations were posted on a bulletin board, telling everyone the prices.

The dollar has since regained its place as the world's key currency, but international acceptance doesn't necessarily mean that everyone agrees on what American money is, particularly since June 24, 1968, when a dollar became unredeemable in three quarters of an ounce of silver. One spokesperson for the U.S. Treasury recently told me, "You can't ask too many questions about money; after a while, it gets very metaphysical." Another stated flatly, "There is no official U.S. government definition of money."

Subsequent calls to the Federal Reserve Board, several Federal Reserve banks, the Comptroller of the Currency, the Secret Service and the Bureau of Printing and Engraving revealed he was essentially correct; however, a government publication entitled "Federal Reserve Glossary" does say that money is "anything that serves as a generally accepted medium of exchange, a standard of value, and a means to save or store purchasing power."

There *is* a definition for "legal tender." According to 31 U.S. Code Section 5103, "all coins and currency of the United States, including Federal Reserve notes, are legal tender for all debts, public charges, taxes and dues." Money is something else, although exactly what, we can't be sure. What is sure is that faith in that money is eroding because of our national credit card, more formally known as the national debt. In *Paper Money,* Adam Smith says, "The building of the debt creates more dollars, which creates a distrust of dollars, which erodes the credibility of the currency as a store of value." Money still buys us what we want when we want it, but lately, barter has been making a comeback precisely at the time paper money is worth less and less; the dollar, for instance, has devaluated 40 percent in the past seventeen years. It stands to reason that as money is worth less, the commodities it will buy are worth more; however, it will take us all some time to adjust to this new reality of commerce, and, after working with cash exclusively, it will take us all a while to get accustomed to thinking of using goods, time and space as substitutes for cash.

One way to overcome the cash-only training we've all been programmed with is to consider barter's efficiency. For example, let's say you're a lawyer who wants to buy a stereo set; you charge $50 an hour and the set costs $500. In the cash world, you would have to find a new client, provide him or her with ten hours of services and collect your fee; that process might take you several months or more. Instead, let's say that you agree to provide $500 worth of legal services directly to the owner of the stereo store in exchange for the set. (I make the basic assumption that both of you law-abiding citizens will declare that income.) You and the stereo retailer are both getting what you want immediately without going through a middleman and without using money as a stopping-off point on the way from your services to his goods and vice versa.

Doing business in this "primitive" way, you're saving the time you would normally spend billing, collecting, depositing, withdrawing and accounting for the cash you would have received or spent and so has the retailer. By any objective standard, the barter method is, in this example, notably cleaner and quicker.

Most corporations talk a good game about wanting to increase efficiency, yet they rarely think or do anything about the time and effort that barter can save when it comes to various aspects of purchasing. Training and force of habit have blinded them to the obvious efficiencies that accompany barter, the medium of payment in which 15 percent of all American business will be done by the year 2000, according to the Stanford Research Institute. Economic trends seem to dictate that, more and more, executives will have to learn to go beyond that increasingly obsolescent form of payment known as money and learn how to do business in a more sophisticated medium—barter.

CHAPTER 3

THE BASICS
OF BARTER

Business? It's quite simple. It's other people's money.
—ALEXANDER DUMAS THE YOUNGER, *La Question d'Argent,* Act II, Scene 7

For the most part, companies barter to solve specific business problems. Even when well-meaning corporations barter for charitable reasons (see Chapter 4), they get economic advantages in the form of tax write-offs. Deciding whether bartering makes sense for you or your company at any given time depends, therefore, on your motivation:

- Is disposing of inventory at the top of your wish list?
- Would increasing your cash flow make your day?
- Are you looking to increase your customer base inexpensively?

Answering these questions will ultimately help you decide on what bartering approach is best in a given situation because in barter the "what" and the "how" are often intertwined.

For example, let's say your number-one priority is to promote old merchandise in order to dispose of it (to make way for a new line); in that case, bartering for media might offer a likely solution to your problem. If you were looking instead to find new buyers for your goods and services, working through a trade exchange or a corporate barter broker might make the most sense. If gaining a

23

marketing presence overseas were paramount, then employing a trading company or working through a countertrade specialist would seem appropriate.

Whichever "how" is most suitable to your "what," the main advantages bartering offers can be grouped under three main headings—finance, purchasing and marketing.

FINANCE: IMPROVE THE BOTTOM LINE

■ **Lower manufacturing costs by bartering production capacity.** You produce a product, and the plant is running at only 80 percent of capacity. (That would be a high figure by most standards.) You approach a barter company about your unused manufacturing capacity, and it asks you to increase production by 5 percent, offering to pay your wholesale costs with TV advertising time. Added costs consist mostly of raw materials, since you're already paying for labor, physical plant costs, insurance and other overhead items anyway. Upping production allows you to lower your unit production costs and get the TV time cheaply to promote your products. B. F. Goodrich has worked deals with Atwood Richards on this basis.

■ **Get a reasonable return for obsolete merchandise.** Everybody makes mistakes, but liquidating your excess inventory for cash generally returns only ten to twenty cents on the dollar. Instead, you can get a dollar-for-dollar credit based on the manufacturing, wholesale or even retail cost of your products, depending on what you are able to negotiate with the barter company. Mattel made a big miscalculation by getting into hand-held calculators; they got out by trading $10 million of inventory in a trade for TV advertising time and billboard space through Deerfield Communications, a corporate broker.

■ **Cut costs of warehousing dead inventory.** Once you've produced an item, it must be stored until it's sold. When it goes unsold too long, you tie up warehousing space and security costs on merchandise that may be unsalable for cash. Moving it through barter channels frees up space for newer merchandise and reduces overall expenses. Yamaha used this method to dispose of unsold motorcycles through 3M's Corporate Trade Center, also in exchange for unsold TV advertising time.

- **Turn inventory into receivables.** The alchemists never did turn lead into gold, but you can turn your excess inventory into receivables—outstanding accounts that can be carried on your books as assets by making a "receivables" deal with a barter company. In such a transaction (explained fully in Chapter 7), you trade your inventory for a credit that is denominated in trade dollars rather than cash. For instance, Diversified Products, a sporting goods manufacturer, traded $4.4 million worth of racquetball equipment and got a receivables credit in that amount, later using it to buy $2.2 million worth of steel, several dozen tractor trailers, $800,000 worth of advertising time and space, rental cars, hotel rooms, printing and office equipment.

- **Transform bad debts into performing assets.** Sometimes creditors take goods instead of cash as a way of settling a debt. When a Mexican customer couldn't repay IC Industries' Abex Corp. $2.5 million, Abex hired a trading company which renegotiated the debt in pesos. According to an aticle in *Forbes,* the pesos were delivered to the trading company's Mexican subsidiary, which bought Mexican products with them, resold them in world markets and delivered the dollars to Abex in New York; the company got the dollars it was owed and also saved executive time and legal fees chasing the bad debt.

- **Borrow less often as a result of increased cash flow.** Even though interest rates are far below 1981 levels, borrowing money is still expensive. By bartering excess capacity for products and services you would normally pay for in cash, you stretch your operating cash and reduce your need to borrow.

PURCHASING: INCREASE YOUR BUYING POWER

- **Conserve cash.** Bartering also allows you to buy in quantities large enough to earn you discounts on items you might have had to pay more for in cash on a unit basis; it can also eliminate the middleman or permit you to make expensive purchases that would have otherwise been impossible. Republic Airlines was able

to buy a $50,000 air compressor by exchanging airline tickets
that it might not have sold for cash anyway.

■ **Use wholesale buying power.** When you barter, you're
generally paying with the wholesale cost of your goods or services. For instance, a survey showed it cost Continental Airlines
only eighteen cents to fly an empty seat. When Continental
wanted hotel rooms for flight crews, it was able to offer New
York's Roosevelt Hotel $300,000 in trade dollars, which, in ef-
fect, cost the corporation only $54,000 on a wholesale basis.

■ **Receive merchandise for resale in company stores.** Obviously, only the largest companies can benefit from this method
of bartering. Nevertheless, 3M uses this as a standard technique,
trading unsold space on advertising billboards for goods its employees can buy at low company store prices. Barter allows 3M to
turn a minus (unsold inventory) into a plus (improved employee
morale).

■ **Pay employees partly with trade dollars.** You can save
cash normally expended on salaries and fringe benefits by com-
pensating employees with noncash payments or using barter to
fund group medical or life insurance plans. In this light, airline
flight passes are a disguised form of barter. AirCal employs a San
Francisco management consultant and pays one third of her bill
with free passes.

■ **Provide valuable incentives.** Rewarding outstanding performance is a necessity for any corporation, but it's a lot less expensive when the reward is funded by barter, not cash. Dispersing
expensive premiums—personal computers, video recorders,
etc.—or rewarding employees, dealers and distributors with fully
paid vacations on a trade basis builds goodwill for companies like
Massey-Ferguson.

MARKETING: CREATE NEW SALES OPPORTUNITIES

■ **Attract new business with minimal sales costs.** When you
sign up with a trade exchange, trading company or a corporate
broker, you are, in effect, increasing your sales staff; they'll sell
your products and services for you, and you'll only pay a small

annual fee plus commissions on actual new business. Xerox Corp. got needed office space by bartering copiers, computers and typewriters; as a bonus, it also attracted new customers it might never have even identified, much less reached through traditional methods.

- **Create a unique marketing advantage.** Barter adds another competitive element to the four traditional criteria of quality, price, delivery and service. You've got a unique competitive edge when you can tell a potential client, "You don't have to pay us in cash." B. F. Goodrich and other companies try to keep their barter arrangements confidential in order to maintain this edge with potential customers.

- **Create noncompetitive channels of distribution.** Once you've decided to dispose of an inventory by selling it at drastically reduced prices, the one situation you want to avoid is having the same merchandise turn up again in your regular sales outlets at bargain basement prices. Shell Oil developed an insect repellent to be used inside metal garbage cans. When plastic bags were introduced, Shell wanted to get rid of its inventory quietly; it was able to exchange five million Can-Care strips for refined sugar from a Caribbean hotel that needed them for pest control.

Naturally, some of these techniques are more applicable to some businesses than others. The travel and media businesses are custom-made for barter because their inventory is so perishable; once an airplane takes off, an empty seat is a dead loss as a source of income, as is an unsold minute of advertising time or an empty hotel room. Some techniques are usable only on a seasonal basis, some have geographical limitations, and some don't work because of industry peculiarities. Most foods, for instance, cannot be bartered because of perishability. Nevertheless, barter can have a positive effect on most businesses, and a thorough knowledge of barter's pluses can suggest new solutions to old problems.

THE DISADVANTAGES

A thorough knowledge of barter's minuses, though, is equally necessary because barter can also create new problems. In 1982 the *Harvard Business Review* warned, "The rapid growth of bartering has been a lure for unscrupulous middlemen who misrepresent the volume of goods and the variety of merchandise available. . . . There have also been complaints of transactions involving damaged or inferior goods, inadequate service, and poor time for advertising on radio and television."

As you can see, most of this negative comment refers to problems associated with spending credits received for bartering goods and services, and for a very good reason: the barter economy is a mirror image of the cash economy. In the cash economy, making a sale and collecting the money is the difficult part, but, once you have the cash, it's easy to spend. In the barter economy, making sales is easy, but finding products and services to spend credits on can be difficult.

The litany of complaints goes like this:

- **"I can never spend my credits."** When a manufacturer has inventory to unload, he or she may take credits without examining too closely just how spendable they really are. Allis-Chalmers and MCA Records are two of the many companies that have been stuck with job lots of unspendable credits as the result of barter deals that didn't work out.

- **"I never get exactly the thing I really want."** One of the realities of bartering is that it's nearly impossible to get *exactly* what you want on a barter basis. Rembrandt etchings and mainframe computers can be sold quite easily for cash, which makes them difficult to come by in the barter marketplace.

- **"I get what I want, but I have to wait forever."** When you pay cash for an item, you generally get immediate delivery. By comparison, barter has a way of teaching patience in an indelible way. When I found Coast Federal Savings was bartering used cars with more than 40,000 miles on them, I put in my order and waited . . . and waited. I finally got what I wanted, but it took me four months of phone calls and reminders.

- **"Everybody inflates their prices on a barter deal."** This is the biggest problem and stems from the attitude that "since barter dollars are not real money, everyone inflates prices because no one needs to be competitive." Of course, inflated prices are no less a problem in the cash world. The only control here is that companies that inflate their prices on barter deals don't get much repeat business.

■ **"I traded for media, and if you happen to be in Pine Bluff, Arkansas at 3 A.M., you can see our new commercial."** Trading for media is a specialty item and should be treated as such. You can't blame the TV station's sales manager for bumping your bartered spots when a cash cutomer walks in. The fact is that most bartered commercials run on an "as available" basis.

■ **"The hotel chain will only let us hold our sales conference in Minneapolis in February."** Bartered meeting room facilities are subject to the same laws of supply and demand as facilities paid for in cash. Naturally, most companies would like to have their sales conference in Miami in February; however, you can often solve the problem by unbundling this two-part package of timing and location and pick a different meeting time or place that will enable you to maximize your credits.

■ **"Every department wants to use the credits."** Even when credits are eminently spendable there are problems, because every department wants to use those wonderful free airline tickets, rental cars, etc. 3M found a way to eliminate this kind of intercompany squabbling: the company set up a system whereby one division earning a barter credit (Magnetic Media, for example) would "sell" airline credits to another (Scotch tape) and take an intracompany credit on its books.

Along with this list of the most general problems with barter, every business person has horror stories that have as much to do with business morality as they do with barter. Such stories don't diminish the usefulness of trading goods and services. As we have seen, barter can contribute to solving a wide range of business problems; any business tool this versatile must inevitably also have its drawbacks.

The barter marketplace is a unique marketplace with many pluses, an equal amount of minuses and a set of unique characteristics:

1. It is almost totally unregulated by the federal government, because it falls between the cracks of the ICC, FTC, Department of Commerce, etc.

2. It is "less real" than cash, which leads to some of the abuses described above.

3. It is practiced amid hushed trappings of secrecy that would do justice to a monastery, because, as currently constituted, barter exists mainly as a blotter to pick up mistakes—marketing shortfalls, overproduction, etc.; few business people like to admit mistakes. (You hadn't noticed?)

And yet, properly practiced, barter can be a tremendous boon to a business. To decide whether or not it can help your business, you'll have to go beyond the pluses and minuses and learn the various methods of trading. Here's a rundown of the most common variations:

▪ **Trading Reciprocally.** You give me this service or product, I give you that one. I once hired an assistant through a search firm, got the firm some national publicity and saved myself a search fee as a result. The advantages are: (1) you know whom you're dealing with, (2) you don't spend a dime, and (3) you're getting the specific item you want. The big drawback is the time you have to invest in finding a trading partner.

▪ **Joining a trade exchange.** Become a member of an exchange, and they'll find a whole new group of local trading partners for you; you may also be able to barter out-of-state, or even internationally; however, (1) it costs a nominal sum to join, (2) you pay commissions when you trade, and (3) you may not be able to spend any or all of your credits.

▪ **Using a corporate broker.** Several new companies that specialize in making barter deals for large corporations rather than local companies have attracted big-name clients like *Playboy* and Yamaha. While they can't guarantee you'll be able to trade for what you want, they may be able to work a three-way trade that will satisfy your needs. The downside? Naturally, their fees are larger, and you're competing for their time and attention with major corporations.

- **Finding a trading company.** A number of *Fortune* 500 companies like K mart, Sears, Roebuck and 3M have actively gone into the business of using their overseas contacts to sell other companies' goods internationally on either a cash or a barter basis. This can be an excellent method to create new distribution channels. (See Chapter 9.) Naturally, many other companies have also become aware of this service, which is why some three-year-old trading companies have as many as 10,000 clients.

- **Trading for real estate, media or travel.** You may be able to defer taxes by bartering real estate, trade excess inventory for broadcasting time, or increase production and swap it to finance your next sales conference. Of course, you may swap for a too-distant condo, get media time when your target audience isn't listening or be forced to schedule your conference or vacation at the hotel's convenience rather than your own. The plus is getting something of value for what may be (to you) worthless inventory.

THE TEN COMMANDMENTS OF BARTER

In the course of making many swaps—good ones and bad ones—I've discovered a few general principles of trading that will apply to most small business owners, corporate executives and professionals. I believe many of the negatives laid at the feet of traders are really the result of their clients' not paying attention to some very basic considerations.

1. **Know why you're trading.** This seems elementary, but trading has a way of igniting elementary passions and causing even the most rational business people to get caught up in the excitement of the process. If your primary objective is conserving cash, stick to it. If you want to make sure products are sold through noncompetitive outlets, stick to it. If you're looking for media, don't get sidetracked with hotel facilities you may not be able to retrade.

2. **Investigate many alternatives.** "Don't put all your eggs in one basket." Working on only a single opportunity makes you more vulnerable to accepting a low offer, because it's the *only*

offer. If you feel trade exchanges are your best bet, talk to three or four of them. If you're unsure about which approach to use, interview several different kinds of companies. Many bartering mistakes can be avoided with some elementary patience. If you give bartering as much thought and care as the other parts of your business, you'll learn quickly how to spot what is truly the best alternative for you.

3. Keep a tight rein on your ego. Marketing robin's-egg-blue catcher's mitts was a fine idea at the time, but that time is past. You made a mistake; your baby is defective. Face it and you may be able to salvage something. Who knows, maybe robin's-egg blue is a hot color in Venezuela.

4. Swap what is truly swappable at the right time and place. Don't try to trade skis in May or roller skates in Samoa. Research alternate distribution outlets for your product thoroughly and then decide on a timing and placement strategy to dispose of your inventory.

5. Maintain realistic goals. Going into the barter marketplace requires the tacit admission that you can't get the cash price you want for your product or services; that's the reason you're bartering. It stands to reason, then, that you should have realistic expectations of what you can get in exchange.

6. Don't try to trade over the telephone. There's a certain amount of chemistry to a trade which doesn't transmit well over phone lines. While talking on the telephone, people can get distracted by office happenings and may turn down what might be a good swap for them as well as for you. Set up a meeting in person, prepare what you're going to say, be persuasive, listen as well as you speak to your trading partners' needs, and you'll make a trade.

7. Don't take rejection personally. Because trading can be an intense and personal experience, novice barterers often get discouraged when their offers are rejected. If you find your first offer rejected, make another one. If your prospective trading partner weren't interested, he or she wouldn't be listening to you in the first place. Sometimes, you can make exactly the same offer but present it a bit differently and wind up making a deal.

8. Use your imagination. If a simple reciprocal swap won't work, try thinking up an alternative that might work—like a three-way deal. For instance, if you've decided to trade scrap steel and are offered rental car vouchers when you really want magazine advertising, it may pay you to take the vouchers in hopes of retrading them later for the print ads you really want. A valuable trading commodity like rental car credits can be "banked" and retraded relatively quickly.

9. Get an outside appraisal of your commodity's worth. A potential trading partner will put greater credence in the *Kelly Blue Book* price for your 1979 Ford Fairlane than your own wild guess. Ask your trading partner for similar information, if possible, in order to provide a starting point for negotiations.

10. Put your deal in contract form. In the afterglow of having successfully negotiated a trade, particularly at the beginning of your bartering career, you may be inclined to take someone's word on a given element of the deal. Resist that impulse. Make the contract as specific as possible. If you agree to trade 5,000 widgets for $5,000 worth of radio time, make sure you specify at what time of day the commercials must run and between what dates they must run to fulfill the contract. Bob Morgan, who ran 3M's trading for eight years and now has his own business, the Corporate Trade Center in Minneapolis, makes the media schedule part of his contracts. Put your deal in contract form and you'll assure yourself of avoiding a common pitfall of bartering.

While there are drawbacks, barter can be imaginative, exasperating, rewarding, ego-deflating, challenging and frustrating—all at the same time. If you want to buy something with cash, you go to a place where it's sold, trade money for it and get it; that's the end of the transaction. When you decide to barter instead, you begin a quest. Basic information will make that quest a bit easier. Now that you have some, it's time to learn how the U.S. government feels about it.

CHAPTER 4

BARTER
AND THE IRS

─────────

When there is an income tax, the just man will pay
more and the unjust less on the same amount of income.
—PLATO, *The Republic*, Book I, 343-D

─────────

Plato wasn't referring to me or you, of course; he was talking
about the other guy. Plato wasn't crazy about him; neither is your
Uncle Sam. For years, some private individuals and companies
have blithely traded goods and services back and forth, while
Uncle stood on the sidelines grumbling about "the underground
economy" and barter's place in it.

In 1982, Uncle stopped grumbling and passed the Tax Equity
and Fiscal Responsibility Act (TEFRA). The act was a compro-
mise, giving Uncle three-part forms and audit trails to confound
tax cheats and, in turn, giving bartering through trade exchanges
official U.S. government recognition as legally authorized economic activity.

Specifically, Section 311 of TEFRA:

- requires trade exchanges to report the bartering of individual
  clients transaction by transaction and to report bartering by
  corporations annually;
- gives barter organizations "third-party record-keeper status," similar to that enjoyed by banks, brokerages and credit
  card companies;

35

- prevents the IRS from summarily summoning records for an audit without notifying the taxpayer involved.

Before TEFRA became law (at the urging of the International Reciprocal Trade Association [IRTA]), trade exchanges, corporate barter brokers and media barterers generally sidestepped the taxation issue. Clients were officially urged to check with their accountants before coming to any determination of taxability (still a good idea); however, unofficially, the line was, "We can't tell you how to handle barter, BUT, the IRS only audits 1.5 percent of all U.S. returns." The implication was that barterers might get away with not declaring income derived from trading, even after the IRS went to court and won the right to subpoena all the records of a given trade exchange through a legal device known as a "John Doe summons."

Of course, bartering itself is quite lawful, its legality recognized under the Uniform Commercial Code which has been adopted by most states. Under the Code, an oral contract (for goods or services under $500) is sufficient to bind both parties, unless a specific inequity won't make it stand up in court; however, even on transactions over $500, there is no legal recourse for the buyer if the goods have been "specially manufactured," or if the goods are paid for and accepted or "received and accepted."

While the IRS has accepted barter's legality it hasn't neglected its taxability. Basically, according to the IRS, income is income, whether it's in cash or in trade; that means—unequivocally—that you or your company must pay taxes on income received through bartering. Sections 1.61-2(d) (1) and (2) of the Internal Revenue Code state that any compensation paid in a medium other than cash, whether paid to an individual or an organization, is includable as income and is taxed at the fair market value of the property or service received.

Fair market value is defined in *Sales and Other Dispositions of Assets,* the 1979 issue of IRS Publication 544, as "the price at which the property would change hands between a willing buyer and a willing seller, neither being under any compulsion to buy or sell, and both having reasonable knowledge of the relevant facts. Assignments of value to the property by parties with adverse interests in an arm's-length transaction are strong evidence of fair market value." (In this context, "arm's length" means "to keep from being friendly or intimate," according to *Funk and Wagnalls Standard College Dictionary*.)

Naturally, one man's fair market value is another's wholesale price; however, there's no room for misinterpretation on another key point. One IRS ruling states unmistakably that credits received through bartering are taxable in the year received, *not* when they are spent. This ruling, the bane of trade exchanges and corporate brokers, means that corporate clients must sometimes report and pay taxes on barter credits even before they're used.

Along with most other Americans, the IRS discovered modern bartering in the 1970s when magazines, newspapers and television began giving the trade exchange concept national exposure. This rush of favorable publicity happened to come at a time when "the underground economy" had become a national catch phrase. Not surprisingly, the IRS put one and one together and decided that trade exchange members were fit subjects for a nationwide investigation.

Under Project Barter, the IRS scrutinized the tax returns of barterers and compared them with returns of nonbartering U.S. taxpayers from October 1979 to June 1981. Initial results showed that 26 percent of 976 selected barterers had no change in their tax liability, more than twice as many as the national average of "no change" audits, which is 12 percent. *Time* reported that Project Barter had netted the government an additional $700,000 in taxes; however, the same survey showed *nonbarterers'* returns averaged additional taxes and penalties of $1,563, while auditing barterers' returns turned up only $556, about a third as much, in additional taxes and penalties.

Largely as a result of Project Barter, the IRTA (then known as the International Association of Trade Exchanges) began lobbying for official recognition of barter. When President Ronald Reagan signed TEFRA in September 1982, Project Barter was abandoned. Since then, the IRS has focused its compliance efforts on trade exchange owners rather than members, particularly the operators who print trade dollars for their own use and don't report them as income.

On May 30, 1984, the U.S. Tax Court ruled that Willis Wright, founder of Unlimited Business Exchange (UBE), had underreported his income from 1976–8 by over $200,000. Wright claimed he had "loaned" himself that much in trade dollars and intended to repay it. Judge William M. Fay decided that since UBE's members "did not know nor did they consent" to his receiving trade units that "exceeded the amount of trade units which had been credited to his account," Wright had created income which he had not declared and was liable for taxes, penalties and interest on it.

The IRS is equally watchful for barter loopholes at the corporate level. Late in 1983 and throughout 1984, "debt-for-equity swaps" briefly became the "hot" new financial instrument. Corporations like Bankers Trust Co., Procter & Gamble and Sears, Roebuck & Co. issued new common stock and used it to retire old notes at low, outdated interest rates. A firm redeeming below-market debt of $100 million with $80 million in stock through a debt (old notes)-for-equity (new stock) swap could book $20 million in instant profits, which is why *Forbes* called such trades "the closest thing to a free lunch that most chief financial officers have ever seen." Unfortunately for these CFOs, the 1984 tax law contained language making debt-for-equity swaps taxable.

Nevertheless, there are other areas of legitimate write-offs and deductions that are made possible by bartering. In one case, a Canadian manufacturer of sporting goods traded $4 million worth of its products to Atwood Richards. The credits were to be used over an eight-month period, even though Atwood doubted it could redeem $4 million worth of credits in so short a time. Atwood didn't know that, at the same time, the sporting goods company was buying another firm which then showed an $8 million profit and, in combination with that transaction, was writing off the Atwood credits as a bad debt. Essentially, the manufacturer put up $4 million in credits against the $8 million profit and only paid tax on the remaining $4 million, which actually amounted to about $2 million in cash. The company had used $4 million worth of off-season skis, $2 million in cash and "creative accounting" to buy an $8 million company.

In a similar vein, Chris Todd, president of Commonwealth Trading Co., a Minneapolis-based sequential trader (see Chapter 7), solved a problem for a client that had invested in a mid-sized manufacturing plant in the Midwest; the plant turned out to be greatly overvalued, and, rather than drastically devalue the plant on its financial statement, the company asked Todd for an alternative; Todd wound up trading the land for products his client could resell—at a loss—and then deduct as expenses rather than write off.

Todd's solution is a variation of what *Forbes* calls "write-down avoidance," using barter to enhance a company's financial statement. It's better known in the barter business as a "receivables deal," a form of balance sheet alchemy that can transform an unsalable inventory into a credit.

Here's an example:

1. Kuppco, a fictitious cup manufacturer, sells an inventory of surplus plastic cups to Swappco, an equally fictitious corporate broker, at their full wholesale price of $100,000.
2. The wholesale value then appears on Kuppco's books as a receivable of $100,000—a credit to be redeemed later in whatever products and services that Swappco can deliver. (Kuppco understands that the credits will expire in a certain period of time, say two years, if they're not used.) Thus, Kuppco avoids the write-down and turns $100,000 in dubious inventory into a $100,000 credit on its books.
3. Kuppco decides to buy cardboard shipping containers through its corporate broker, and Swappco says, "The containers regularly cost $50,000, but because of our buying power, we're able to get them for you at $30,000." Kuppco says, "Fine. I'll take them."
4. Kuppco pays $30,000 in cash for the containers—the

price Swappco was able to negotiate—plus $20,000 in credits—the difference between the regular price and the negotiated price—which is then deducted from its credit line with Swappco. In addition, Swappco will rebate to Kuppco a percentage of the cash it receives from liquidating the cups and deduct that as well from Kuppco's credit line.

The advantages are (1) that the inventory can be written off the books immediately by being used as expenses, (2) the company is using unsold cups to buy containers it needs, and (3) Swappco is taking responsibility for liquidating the cups and returning a portion of the cash. (In a real-world example, Nike was able to negotiate a 60 percent rebate on an inventory of obsolete footwear with its corporate broker.)

If all the credits are spendable, everything is rosy; however, the disadvantage is that some receivables deals are never completed because the credits remain unspent by the expiration date of the contract. For instance, MCA Records made a receivables deal with Deerfield Communications for 1.2 million records and cassettes, which were assigned a value of $2 million in credits. In the first nine months, MCA was only able to use up $100,000 worth.

Such uncertainty has led various accountants, lawyers and consultants to find a surer, and even more deductible way to write off an inventory—give it away. When donated to charity, such "gifts-in-kind" qualify as "inventory donations" under sec. 170 (e) (3) of the Internal Revenue Code. The section specifies that "the sum of the employer's basis (i.e., cost) in the property plus one half of the unrealized appreciation (profit) is deductible." In other words, on goods manufactured in the United States,

Cost plus 50 percent of profit equals deduction.

Let's say that a computer company builds a computer at a cost of $500 which sells at retail for $1,500. Under a gift-in-kind donation, the company is allowed to deduct $500 (its basis) plus

another $500 (one half the cost of the $1,000 unrealized appreciation). Thus, it would get a $1,000 write-off for an item that
cost it $500 to produce. That helps explain why Apple Computer,
Inc. gives away 1,200 personal computers annually, and IBM is
giving $40 million worth of computers to twenty-two universities
over three years.

Of course, many socially responsible corporations give products, services and real estate to deserving charities with no deductible strings attached. For example, the Conference Board
reported that $86 million was given by corporations in 1984 with
no deductions taken due to the paperwork involved; however, the
deductible variety of gifts-in-kind is growing and amounted to
nearly $100 million in 1982.

3M has given away $24.5 million worth of typewriters and
copiers to the United Negro College Fund and the United Way,
which has set up a separate organization called Gifts in Kind in
Alexandria, Virginia, to distribute in-kind gifts through 2,200
local United Way organizations. Similarly, the National Association for the Exchange of Industrial Resources (NAEIR) in Chicago annually distributes $40 million worth of goods and
services—components from Westinghouse, typewriter ribbons
and liquid paper from Gillette and microscopes from Welch Sci-
entific Instrument Co.—to 4,000 not-for-profit organizations in
every state of the country.

REAL ESTATE EXCHANGES: SECTION 1031

While barter makes the above-mentioned tax deductions and
write-offs possible, real estate exchanging—swapping one piece
of property for another—affords a perfectly legal way of deferring taxes, sometimes indefinitely.

This financial wizardry comes courtesy of Section 1031 of the
Internal Revenue Code. In the 1960s, surging California land
prices led to equally skyrocketing tax bites for people who sold
their property. Of necessity, some California real estate agents
and tax planners began combing the IRS regulations for a real estate loophole and found it in Section 1031, which had actually

been on the books since the 1934 revision of the Internal Revenue Code.

It reads, "No gain or loss shall be recognized if property held for productive use in a trade or business or for investment is exchanged solely for property of like-kind to be held either for productive use in trade or business or for investment." The word spread quickly, and 1031 has subsequently become an important tool for realtors, estate managers, tax consultants, and pension fund administrators all over the United States.

There are several specific exceptions to 1031. Robb Giannangeli, public affairs manager of the IRS in Los Angeles, points out that, under 1031 (a)(2) the deferral specifically does not apply to "stock in trade (i.e., inventory); stocks, bonds or notes; interest in a partnership or any other securities or evidence of indebtedness" (ruling out a tax deduction for banks which constantly swap mortgages, itself a $700 billion business in 1984). On the other hand, Professor Michael P. Sampson, director of the University of Baltimore's Graduate Tax Program, says when 1031 is used correctly, "What you get is an interest-free loan from the federal government (on your untaxed profits) for as long as you want one."

Cliff Johnson of American Real Estate Exchange (AMREX) in Foster City, California, explains how it works: "Let's say you bought a piece of property in 1945 for $100, and it later becomes the site of a major development worth $500,000. You can exchange it for a property worth $2 million and use the value of your original building as a down payment; now you owe $1.5 million but you pay no taxes. The *basis* of your tax is the amount of money you paid decreased by the amount of depreciation. If you keep taking out loans on the property, you never have to pay capital gains tax."

Just as with inventory donations (gifts-in-kind), "basis" is the key word; your basis is your cost, with minor adjustments. With real estate, your basis rises as your property *appreciates* through improvements and *depreciates* as more and more of it is written off. For example, a syndicate of Los Angeles dentists buys a building for $400,000, which is worth $1 million ten years later.

The syndicate is interested in another building also worth $1 million. If it has already written off $200,000 for depreciation, its cost basis is now $200,000. On a sale of the first building, its taxable profit would be $800,000.

However, *in a like-kind exchange, the new property takes on the cost basis of the old property.* If the syndicate buys the new building, its cost basis will be the sale price—$1 million; if it swaps one property for the other, its cost basis is still only $200,000, thus deferring—not eliminating—taxes on $800,000. (This example assumes that either both buildings were free and clear of any mortgages or that the amounts of existing mortgages were even.)

As to what constitutes a like-kind real estate exchange, if the purpose of ownership is similar, the exchange is like-kind; that means an apartment house can be traded for a condo or a shopping center if investment is the reason for the exchange. Giannangeli points out that "like-kind refers to the nature or character of the property and not to its grade or quality" and adds that, for example, "exchanges of livestock of different sexes do not constitute like property."

Despite these exceptions, 1031 has wide application in real estate. One such exchange enabled Dallas-based Trammell Crow Corp. (TCC) to built a mixed-use retail, commercial and condominimum project in the expensive Georgetown section of Washington, D.C. TCC had discovered a 95,000-square-foot lumberyard a mere block away from Georgetown's hottest shopping district; unfortunately, the owner of the lumber yard didn't want to sell because selling would have involved a seven-figure tax liability. Subsequent investigation showed, however, that he did want (1) a suburban location, ideally near a railroad siding; (2) long-term income; (3) depreciable real estate; and (4) some cash.

Armed with that "want list," TCC bought a 70 percent interest in a downtown Washington office building and seventeen acres of industrially-zoned land in suburban Virginia—with a railroad spur, no less. When TCC added an undisclosed amount of cash ("boot" in 1031 terminology), the exchange was completed. The owner got a seven-acre site for his yard, ten adjoining acres for future expansion and a tax-sheltered cash flow from the office building, all with a negligible tax liability; TCC got 95,000 square feet in the middle of Georgetown.

What's more, 1031 exchanges are flexible; they can be geographically separated, sequential, and separated by time in that one part of a transaction can be delayed. The delayed exchange passed an important court test in *Starker v. U.S. 602 F 2d 1341 9th Cir. 1979*. Starker had transferred title of some timber land to Crown Zellerbach Corp.; instead of receiving anything immediately, however, he merely received a credit usable for like-kind property at a future date. The IRS attacked Starker's tax treatment of the swap because the parties didn't exchange properties at the same time; the appellate court, however, ruled in Starker's favor on the grounds that simultaneous transactions were not necessary for the deal to qualify as a Section 1031 exchange.

On the other hand, the IRS recently won a victory that has bearing on such exchanges. The 1984 Tax Reform Act requires that an exchangor must now specifically identify the other half of his or her exchange within forty-five days after the escrow period ("the closing") to keep deferring taxes. In addition, instead of being able to complete a swap in an indefinite period of time, an exchangor now must complete the exchange within 180 days after the forty-five-day period or before the deadline for his or her next tax return. Thus, the new provision precludes exchanges that are, in reality, fishing expeditions.

A potential 1031 exchange or any other barter-related deduction or write-off should be discussed thoroughly with a lawyer, accountant or tax consultant because of the many quirks in the 6,000-page Internal Revenue Code. Secondly, a deduction that is allowable for federal income tax returns may not be permissible on a given state return since the fifty states often differ markedly in their tax treatment of specific transactions. Finally, it's possible that President Reagan's proposed tax simplification plan will change the taxability of some of the techniques mentioned above. Make sure of your facts before claiming a deduction or writing off an inventory. The cost of expert up-front advice may be high, but it may save you many times that fee in the long run.

Now that you know how the federal government feels about barter, it's time to combine your knowledge of the barter basics and IRS interpretations with details of the various methods of trading, starting with the baseball card method—reciprocal trade.

CHAPTER 5

RECIPROCAL
TRADING

In matters of commerce the fault of the Dutch is offering too little and asking too much.
—British statesman GEORGE CANNING

Canning put his finger on the basic problem with reciprocal trading, which is also known as "heads-up" or "one-on-one trading" because it involves two parties directly trading one product or service for another. The process is simplicity itself, except for the problem of valuation. Since there are no *Kelly Blue Books* for fad clothing or pool equipment, what's your pool cover worth? What's my raccoon coat worth? What's anything worth?

Once the dollar or any other currency is eliminated as a standard of measure, reciprocal traders are left with a pure barter situation. Things haven't changed much since 42 B.C. when Publilius Syrus said, "Everything is worth what its purchaser will pay for it."

Oddly enough, Soviet bloc countries have found a way to address this problem: they use dollar prices—even with each other. One Eastern economist jokingly suggests that, even after the "inevitable" world revolution, Moscow will find it necessary to preserve one capitalist country. "Otherwise," he says, "how will we know at what prices to trade?"

The answer for the Russians and for any other would-be swappers lies in finding a starting point. When you and I decide to trade, we begin by assigning an arbitrary value to our own pos-

47

session, the figure we personally think it's worth; the true value of your item to me or mine to you will only later become established when more information is exchanged.

During negotiations, you discover my raccoon coat cost $140 in 1927 and has a one-inch hole under the left sleeve, ". . . but it doesn't show if you stand like Bear Bryant." I find out that your pool cover cost $200 in 1983, but it's square, while my pool is oval. Using some basic fairness and common sense, we negotiate back and forth and eventually agree to trade the coat for the cover, because each of us would rather have an item we can really use, rather than one which merely uses up precious storage space.

In my own direct trades, I've found that sometimes you give greater value than you receive, and sometimes it's the other way around. I once found an assistant through a search firm; ordinarily, I would have paid a fee of $700; instead, I was able to get the personnel firm featured in a national magazine, which was probably worth $3,000. On another occasion, I traded my copywriting services for computer supplies and, for an hour of my time, got $400 worth of printer ribbons; it all evens out.

In personal trading utility is the prime factor, but, naturally, in the business world the profit motive overrides other considerations. When you traded baseball cards as a kid and got stuck with three copies of Harry Chiti, that was just unfortunate; when four different general managers in the real world traded Babe Ruth, Cy Young, Tris Speaker and Lefty Grove for a mortgage, a suit of clothes, a rental fee and a center field fence respectively, they each went hunting for a new line of work.

Despite this hardball aspect of heads-up trading, other, mutually beneficial trades occur all the time. For instance:

- The *Chicago Tribune* lowers its freight costs by supplying complimentary copies to Western Airlines.
- Avon Products swapped $4 million worth of cosmetics to the Soviet Union for Russian crystal and china and plans to use them as bonuses for its sales force.
- According to *Editor & Publisher,* the trade magazine for newspapers, 1,424 farmers in Hutchinson, Kansas, swap

wheat every year for subscriptions to the *Hutchinson News.*
- Republic Airlines swapped airline tickets for land owned by Pillsbury Corp. in a Chicago suburb.

Rewarding performance and conserving cash are laudable goals, and thousands of other barter-minded companies conclude similar transactions every day. But now, some trade-oriented corporations are applying the principles of reciprocal trading in more innovative ways.

Among other things, professionals, small companies and large corporations can use direct barter to:

- **promote products inexpensively.** A number of corporations, large and small, trade their products and services for promotional mentions through media. On the simplest level, this can take the form of "The tenth caller on our WSFX hotline wins dinner for two at Alphonse's Restaurant." It can also serve as a substitute for national television advertising, as in "Promotional consideration provided by Hilton Hotels."

- **increase equity.** Rather than charge cash for their services, professionals have occasionally traded that expertise for a piece of the action. *The Wall Street Journal* reported that, in 1982, Massachusetts attorney Dennis O'Connor bartered his legal services for five percent of Ivy Microcomputer, Inc. When the company went public in May 1984, his share was worth $400,000.

- **solve problems.** We saw earlier that real estate exchanges in compliance with Section 1031 of the Internal Revenue Code could defer capital gains taxes. Other business people have used real estate swapping to solve a host of financial problems. For instance, when the late Carroll Rosenbloom wanted to move to California, he swapped the Baltimore Colts for the Los Angeles Rams using real estate exchanging as the mechanism.

PROMOTING PRODUCTS INEXPENSIVELY

As noted, reciprocal trades of products for advertising services—on-air mentions, billboards, newspaper space—can be made at the very local level for small retail businesses. In many cases, advertising salespeople will throw in a promotional sweetener to make a deal. "If you'll buy a thirteen-week contract, we'll create a contest to give away cruise tickets and mention your travel agency six times a day as a bonus."

While there are limits to this kind of thing (after all, how many refrigerators can you give away?), companies, particularly those selling luxury items, promote themselves by swapping products for services all the time. Since 1962, Blackglama has used the world's best-known and most glamorous women—Liza Minnelli, Diana Ross, Lauren Bacall—as models in endorsement ads; the women allow themselves to be photographed in exchange for the gift of a Blackglama mink. Similarly, a Ford TV spot featured models in Eddie Bauer clothing; in return, Bauer gave Ford a page in his catalog and displayed Ford brochures in his retail outlets.

These are traditional uses for reciprocal trading, but others are less conventional. Peter Ueberroth became *Time*'s man of the year in 1984, in part by putting a new twist on reciprocal trading. In years prior to the summer games in Los Angeles, the Olympics had worked to attract nearly two hundred "official sponsors" and charged strictly cash fees for such rights. Instead, Ueberroth reconsidered the awarding of sponsorships as a way of reducing operational expenses rather than as a way of increasing revenues and cut the number of sponsors down to twenty-four.

Corporations supported the idea enthusiastically; Levi's contributed 10,000 outfits of clothing and Fuji film donated 250,000 rolls of film plus processing. While some sponsors put up as much as $4–$13 million in cash rather than merchandise for their sponsorships, Brother Industries laid out no money but became the official typewriter for the Olympics in exchange for 1,000 machines. By using sponsorships and barter to reduce expenses rather than increase revenues, Ueberroth wound up with the largest cash surplus in Olympics history.

Trading products for promotion was new to the Olympics, but a dozen firms in New York and Los Angeles donate their clients' props to the movies every day and turn that service into cash.

Firms like Unique Product Placements of North Hollywood, California, place products in major motion pictures for clients that include IBM, Levi's and Honda, while Mercedes-Benz, Coca-Cola, Pepsico and Anheuser-Busch assign in-house executives to the task.

Other firms render similar services for television exposure. Such deals are a combination of product cost and cash fee; the higher the retail value, the lower the cash fee, which can get as low as zero for a high-priced item like a computer, making the product for promotion swap a heads-up trade. *Madison Avenue* magazine says that promoting a candy bar on the highly rated nighttime version of *Family Feud* might cost $2,000 for ten seconds as opposed to $40,000 for a regular thirty-second commercial.

Offering money and merchandise doesn't guarantee exposure, however. Unglamorous products like bug sprays, premixed concrete and generators don't make it onto the small screen. Those that do are promoted in discrete "spots" known as ten-second ID's (identifications), complete with an announcer's pitch in twenty-five words or less and seven to ten seconds of visual exposure. Advertisers can now control the quality of their spots by submitting videotape to producers. As the practice of swapping product for promotion has become more sophisticated, it has also grown beyond the boundaries of game shows. *Hour Magazine, American Bandstand, Family* and *NFL Week in Review* are other TV shows that use products for "promotional considerations."

CREATING EQUITY

Professionals and other individuals, who are generally paid on a fee basis, often have the opportunity to forgo those cash payments in search of bigger game; instead of cash, they will often accept equity in their client's company and hope that the stock will take off, ultimately returning far more than the fee they would normally have charged.

The effectiveness of this technique goes back to at least the 1850s when lawyer Edward Clark took a percentage of Isaac Singer's sewing machine company as payment for representing him against other owners of sewing machine patents like Elias Howe. Singer, Howe and two other patent owners had battled for years over royalties. In October, 1854, Clark persuaded all the claimants to create the Sewing Machine Combination, a patent pool which earned royalties for each inventor on every sewing machine produced thereafter.

Clark and Singer parted ways in 1863, each getting 2,075 of the company's 5,000 shares and selling the remaining 850 for $200 apiece, giving them each $85,000 in cash. Members of the Clark family have remained major shareholders of the resultant Singer Manufacturing Co. ever since. One of Clark's shares, adjusted for subsequent stock splits and dividends, had become 900 shares worth $36,000 by 1958 and had paid cash dividends of $131,340, according to *American Heritage,* making Clark's original barter investment worth $347 million at that time.

The possibility of duplicating such seductive success has even attracted the world's largest executive search firm. Korn/Ferry International, with thirty-five offices in fifteen countries and annual revenues of $50 million, began a specialty division called Vensearch in 1983. While Korn/Ferry client searches usually involve familiar companies like Merrill Lynch and Occidental Petroleum and large cash fees (one third of an executive's annual salary), their Vensearch clients, which are largely unknown, pay instead with equity in their companies.

Thus far, Buzz Schulte, the San Francisco–based originator of the Vensearch idea, says the company has made such arrangements with twenty-five companies, 80 percent in various high-technology ventures, which meet three criteria: 1) the company must be privately held; 2) it must offer long-term growth; 3) Vensearch clients must be thriving with a "healthy base of funds." Korn/Ferry won't commit to a Vensearch arrangement unless a "reputable financing source" has already done extensive research on the company.

Schulte is upbeat about the program's long-term benefits in building stable client relationships. "It's an interesting way of creating a long-range client base, particularly since most of the people we recommend are in senior positions of management." So far, all Vensearch companies are thriving, and clients include a . satellite photography firm which locates mineral deposits and companies in medical diagnostics, lens coatings and film head technology, and several have gone public, giving Korn/Ferry potentially valuable stock.

There's a downside to all this, though; offering services for equity is admittedly a gamble. Ron Rogers, head of Rogers & Cowan, a large Los Angeles PR firm, has gambled services for equity three times. The first—and worst—experience involved a ski manufacturer, all of whose companies are currently bankrupt and being administered by courts. Rogers says, "I've got the world's only $20,000 pair of skis."

He's done a little better with Arktronics, a software company, and is currently its fourth-largest stockholder. Rogers hopes his third venture involving trading services for equity will be the luckiest of all. He's one of four founders of a new company called Paradise Cuisine International, Ltd., and all four are bartering their expertise for an equity share in McQueen's Natural Dairy-Free Frozen Dessert, which Carnation will manufacture and Dreyer's will distribute.

Some people do so well with service-for-equity swaps that they wind up suggesting them instead of merely agreeing to them. It happened that way with Janice Jones, president of Chartwell & Co., an investment and financial services firm in Los Angeles. Jones, who originally studied industrial psychology, has traded her financial savvy for pieces of more than forty companies, and her holdings have a current market value of $15 million.

Jones gambled her student loan money in the stock market, and, after a string of losses, her stock broker picked a winner—high-tech Haber Instruments. Jones began touting the stock to potential investors, talking up its potential, and shared the wealth when it grew from one dollar to eighty-eight dollars a share over ten years. When founder Norman Haber found out about Jones's enthusiastic marketing efforts, he hired her to promote his stock to a national audience of investors.

After working with Haber and a six-year hitch at a New York investor relations firm, Jones began Chartwell and viewed bartering for equity as a way of "getting into the venture business without any cash." She decided to offer her marketing services to start-up firms in exchange for equity. Her biggest success so far is a company called Cyanotech, which converts algae into fertilizer. Its stock rose in price from "just pennies" to eighty-five cents a share, a bonanza for Jones, since Chartwell owns 600,000 shares and she owns two million shares personally.

SOLVING PROBLEMS

We've already seen in previous chapters how Abex used barter to collect a problem debt (turning it into products salable for cash) and how Section 1031 real estate swaps defer taxation. Every day, 20,000 people in the United States combine these two uses of barter to solve a host of financial problems and defer tax liabilities for individuals and corporations by swapping real estate. They're called real estate exchangors, are accredited and swap an estimated $25 billion worth of real estate annually.

By the judicious swapping of private homes, shopping centers, vacant lots and vacation homes, they can increase their clients' cash flow, provide for retirement income, reduce living expenses, set up tax shelters and dispose of problem properties. The range of problems they solve can be illustrated by these examples:

■ **Expansion**—Teledyne Microelectronics of Marina Del Rey, California, needed land adjacent to it for expansion; their neighbor needed more land for a plant as well as some income property. A real estate exchangor found the solution; Teledyne bought two properties in California—a shopping center located in Covina and a plant in Chatsworth—and traded them to its neighbor for the adjoining land.

■ **Currency problems**—The owner of a plantation in Argentina wanted to sell his investment for cash, but Argentina, like many countries, doesn't allow currency to leave its borders. A real estate exchangor swapped his client's plantation for a neighbor's and made the form of payment a presold boatload of bananas coming into Los Angeles harbor.

■ **Reinvestment**—A real estate syndicator who owned forty-seven four-unit apartment houses in San Jose, California, wanted to sell them and, in turn, buy shopping centers in high-growth areas, but didn't have any spare cash. San Diego exchangor Chet Allen pulled off a Rube Goldberg swap, eventually involving thirty-five principals, fourteen brokers and twelve lenders in a sixty-three-property exchange; his client wound up with shopping centers in Jacksonville, Tucson and Boise worth a total of $13,888,000.

Along with colorful deals, exchangors have developed equally colorful jargon. Each party to a trade is referred to as a leg; thus, a "three-leg" trade involves three parties. The "upleg" is the more highly valued property; the "downleg," or "downstroke," the less valuable. A "refinancing crank" is not a nasty banker but rather a way to take cash out of a property by refinancing it. Notes and mortgages are "paper," and "paper that walks backward" is a loan in which the principal *increases* every year. An "alligator" eats money, but some properties are only "lizards," because they eat less; others involve so much "eat"—negative cashflow—they are "zoos." A "sandwich" is property you have leased from one party and then re-leased to another at a higher figure; "ice box land" is land of such minimal value that its sole function is to hold the landscape together.

Exchangors deal in "lizards" and "sandwiches" one-on-one and also swap at annual events like the Real Estate Expo, which attracts 3,000 attendees to Las Vegas and has generated as much as $200 million worth of trades in five days; however, most exchanges occur as the result of regular "marketing meetings." Every exchangor who attends such meetings contributes ideas, giving the gathering some of the air of a group therapy session.

One exchangor describes what he does as "economic psychoanalysis," and exchangors routinely ask their clients for tax returns and health records to get the information they need to solve a problem and make a deal.

On November 1, 1984, thirty-nine members of the San Fernando Valley Exchangors, a division of the National Council of Exchangors, held their monthly marketing meeting. Eleven "packages" were presented for exchanging, including:

- a shopping center in Hawthorne ($500,000);
- a five-bedroom house in Laurel Hills ($355,000);
- eight apartments in Van Nuys ($380,000);
- a 6,000-square-foot lot in Del Mar ($259,000).

The lot in Del Mar is free and clear, has an unobstructed view of a state park and belongs to a forty-year-old architect who bought it as a home site but who was later transferred to Los Angeles. After digesting the problem, members presented broker Jay MacIntosh of Merrill Lynch Realty with four different ideas: (1) create a joint venture with a builder; (2) have her client's architectural firm buy the lot and build on it and, in exchange, find him a house in Los Angeles; (3) sell the lot to a "spec" (speculative) home builder who builds homes in the $600,000 range; and, (4) list the house with three other San Diego exchange groups.

Since every member can only suggest one package at each meeting, members are free to list other properties on a wall known as "the Country Store." Sometimes, these parcels are used as "can-adds" (sweeteners) or become catalysts for other deals. After all the packages have been presented, members can present unwanted non–real estate items—watches, jewelry, pleasure boats, mink coats, horses—at a "cowboy auction." While members like to think of real estate exchanging as something totally apart from bartering, they swap with obvious relish.

Real estate exchanging works because it involves a personal touch and a problem-solving approach generally absent from land deals negotiated on a cash basis. There's also a third and very practical reason for its existence: exchanging makes more deals possible because there's more equity out there than there is money.

THE PLUSES AND MINUSES OF RECIPROCAL TRADING

Reciprocal trading in these specialized and the more mundane areas is a relatively easy way to get some on-the-job training in barter for the following reasons:

1. You know whom you're dealing with, which makes for fewer unpleasant surprises, fewer misunderstandings and smoother relations during the trading process.

2. With only two parties involved, information, a key commodity in barter negotiations, doesn't get misconstrued, overblown or underplayed as often.

3. Both parties display a desire to trade early in the process, saving a lot of time and obviating the usual posturing.

4. Generally speaking, reciprocal trades occur mostly when one party wants a specific product or service he knows the other has. This factor makes the swap a positive experience compared with a situation where you're trying to get rid of a dead inventory through a third party; in that instance, you're trading for *anything* rather than something specific.

5. Since many business people who trade reciprocally have an ongoing relationship, keeping the long-term picture in view provides for greater honesty, better follow-through and more conciliation on both sides.

On the other hand, there are some negatives attached to even this most simple bartering method.

1. Distribution can be a problem in reciprocal trades. A pharmaceutical company got rid of some inventory, stipulating that it be sold offshore. It was shipped to England, then reappeared in America six weeks later in the manufacturer's regular outlets at a cut-rate price.

2. Shipping and warehousing can cause more problems in barter situations. One barterer recalls trading broadcast advertising time for 50,000 appliances which were supposed to be deliv-

ered in original factory-sealed cartons and were released against receipts as specified in a letter of credit; only 20,000 were factory sealed, and the recipient voided the letter of credit, necessitating a costly settlement. In another case, a golf shirt manufacturer was supposed to ship six shirts to a box—two large, two medium, one small and one extra large; they came four to a box in mixed sizes, causing cancellation of the contract.

3. Even though the trade only involves two parties, others often become involved. Republic Airlines made an irrevocable $45,000 trade with a western hotel to put up two flight crews; the deal involved shifting the crews from their favorite hotel, albeit upgrading them to better accommodations five minutes farther from the airport. The pilots' union called, claiming the company was endangering passengers' lives by depriving the pilots of eight hours sleep, and, to reinforce the point, two pilots "overslept," necessitating ninety-minute delays in departures.

The airline canceled the contract, the hotel threatened to sue. Eventually, Republic had to eat $24,000 worth of tickets; the word "irrevocable" was stricken from future contracts. Dennis Needham, who once headed Republic's in-house barter unit, explains, "Each department has favorite vendors, hotels, restaurants, etc., just like the pilots. You may think you've become a hero and saved the company money at the same time, but you may find the people you're helping are fighting you behind your back."

FOUR WAYS TO IMPROVE YOUR RECIPROCAL TRADES

These examples are proof positive that, even with proper planning, things can still go wrong in a reciprocal trade; on the other hand, similar things go wrong in other forms of barter as well as the cash marketplace all the time. There is nothing inherent in a barter deal that makes it better or worse than a cash deal; however, it does pay to give your first barter deals more thought, care and preparation, just because they are the first.

1. **Expand your concept of inventory.** What you have to

trade goes beyond actual physical objects sitting on shelves. Think of time as an element of inventory. (Broadcasters do.) If you're a professional, barter can fill the unbilled time in your schedule; if you're a manufacturer, your unused production time can be bartered. Think of space as an element of inventory as well. (Hotels and airlines do.) You may be able to warehouse someone else's excess inventory in exchange for something you need.

2. Keep organized "have" and "want" lists. In addition to what you can personally offer in trade, keep a record of other items you know about that are available for trade. You may not actually need 190,000 tons of frozen boysenberries, but, if you found that a frozen foods company did, the information would come in very handy. Up-to-date lists (particularly computerized ones) can help you seize trading opportunities when they do arise.

3. "Sell" what you have to trade. Every trade is actually a sale in disguise; only the method of payment is different. Sell what you have to offer just as aggressively as you would selling it for cash. It's a mistake to think that the payment medium changes the tone of your message. Describe what you want to trade as compellingly as possible and make sure you outline all its possible benefits to your trading partner.

4. Never negotiate from weakness. Don't even begin to discuss a reciprocal trade (or any other kind) unless you are sure about your facts and feel that what you have to offer is a good opportunity for your trading partner. Negotiation generally involves strain and stress; not having confidence in your research or the value of your offer may cause you to rush over sticky points that will come back to haunt you. Postpone the swapping session until you're feeling positive on all counts.

Once you've mastered the ins and outs of trading one-on-one, you'll have a clear idea of how the trading process works as opposed to a cash transaction. You'll also know what's involved for third-party barterers, because all the other varieties of barter involve them, as we shall see. Before considering the most complex third-party deals—media, travel and countertrade, we'll examine the simplest—the trade exchange.

CHAPTER 6

TRADE EXCHANGES:
LOCAL BARTER BROKERS

Commerce has passed through five stages. It started with barter, then came coins, paper currency and credit cards. Now, more and more, it's going back to barter.
—MARVIN J. "MAC" McCONNELL

Reciprocal trading is the simplest form of barter, but working through a trade exchange runs it a close second. As we have seen, reciprocal trading involves two buyers and two sellers, which make, in all, two parties because each is simultaneously involved on both ends of the trade.

A trade exchange, on the other hand, involves three parties—two buyer-sellers and a trader. What's more, as noted earlier, the buyer-sellers don't swap with each other. Instead, they swap indirectly; they put products and services into the system and earn credits, then spend them on other goods and services put into the system by other members.

Exchange members read about availabilities in the directory or newsletter published by the exchange. (The smartest ones also keep up relationships by calling regularly.) When a trade broker suggests a purchasing opportunity, the member is free to accept or reject it; however, some trade exchanges mandate a minimal amount of trading activity within a year's time to cover their administrative expenses.

When a member does decide to put goods or services into the system, he or she gets a direct, immediately spendable credit equal to the amount of products or services he trades minus a sales commission. For instance, if a manufacturer trades office furniture worth $10,000 at retail, he might get a $9,500 credit in trade dollars and pay a $500 commission to the trade exchange. Some exchanges divide the 10 percent fee in half and charge 5 percent commissions on all sales and 5 percent commissions on all purchases, but the difference is cosmetic; by the time you buy something, you will have paid a 10 percent commission under either system.

Most trade exchanges issue plastic credit cards to their members and require authorizations over a set amount, generally fifty dollars. Some systems have their seller members call headquarters; others use an 800 telephone number. All transactions are recorded on multiple-copy forms, like those used by Visa or MasterCard, and copies are sent to the buyer, the seller and, eventually, the exchange's copy goes to the IRS.

When professionals and businesses consider the pluses and minuses of trade exchange membership, they weigh the costs of fees and commissions plus the extra time involved in working through a trade exchange against the value of signing up new customers they wouldn't otherwise meet and the use of excess inventory to make purchases (allowing them to conserve cash).

It's true that such local retail transactions might also have been accomplished by reciprocal trading, but it would have taken a bit more luck and a lot more time. If you wanted to seek out a specific item for use in a reciprocal trade, you'd have to invest a lot of legwork to find out if it were even available. The biggest advantage of working through a trade exchange lies in its clearinghouse function, which makes it easy for an accountant to buy carpeting without having to devote his time and energy to finding a carpeting company willing to trade for his specific services.

Membership in a trade exchange is especially valuable for professionals—lawyers, doctors, accountants, insurance brokers. For these people, free time consists of the time they haven't been able to fill with billable work for clients; therefore, getting something for their time—goods and/or services—is far better than getting nothing at all.

It's almost as effective for small-service businesses for much the same reason—getting new business. Dry cleaners and other similar providers of strictly local services can't get much benefit from advertising or commissioned salespeople; therefore, getting new customers on a trade basis enlarges their customer base, and providing good service may keep them, even on a cash basis.

When the franchised trade exchange boom began, interstate bartering became a reality, and, for the first time, trade exchange owners were approaching companies like Xerox, B. F. Goodrich and Continental Airlines and signing them up. Giants like these found that they too could benefit from membership in a trade exchange. As noted, Xerox got needed office space for used copiers, Goodrich got a company plane in exchange for surplus tires, and Continental put up flight crews with credits earned from bartered tickets.

Major corporations, like professionals and small businesses, were attracted because trade exchanges combine four important business functions. They provide a clearinghouse for goods and services; broker those goods and services to members; act as bankers by providing a currency—trade dollars; and control the accounting system by issuing credits and debits. All three classes of business were able to utilize the trade exchange's most important function, that of providing the clearinghouse. (Some exchanges talk of themselves as being "banks that store goods and services rather than money.") The exchange hires salespeople (generally on commission) to sign up members, large and small, then assigns trade brokers (account executives) to call up specific clients when items they had requested earlier become available.

Naturally, trade brokers also call when items of general interest become available, because trade exchanges only make money three ways—through initiation fees ($300 is a good average), annual renewal fees (generally $100), and commissions on each trade, usually 10 percent.

Back in the 1970s, trade exchanges used to say, "If you can't trade for it, you don't need it." In line with that philosophy, most collected their commissions wholly in trade dollars. As time went on, that system proved impractical since trade exchanges must pay taxes, utilities and other overhead items in cash, just like other businesses; most adopted a policy of half cash, half trade early in the 1980s.

Generally speaking, "transaction fees" are now payable all in cash. Since commissions represent by far the largest part of the income of independent trade exchanges (those not tied into a nationally franchised chain), it's in their interest to keep finding new products and services for their members to trade, leading to more commissions.

As if providing the clearinghouse and a closely related business brokerage weren't enough, trade exchanges also decided to act as bankers. Instead of denominating credits and debits earned through their auspices in U.S. currency, playing cards, tobacco, cattle or beads, they administer a private currency called trade dollars (or trade units or trade credits). Each unit bears the name of its sponsoring exchange, hence the "BX dollar" for the currency of Business Exchange, or "BEI credit" for the trade dollar earned through Barter Exchange, Inc. Extending the analogy, some exchanges pay interest on positive balances over a certain limit; others offer loan services and accept monthly payments in merchandise, promised services or trade dollars.

What do these broker-purchaser-bankers do in their spare time? When they're not signing clients, adding goods and services or supervising their banking business, trade exchanges also act as accounting systems. With the help of the ubiquitous computer, they figure out each member's balance, assigning credits and debits and mailing out monthly statements to members as well as regular reports of transactions to the Internal Revenue Service. In fact, the accounting portion of the trade exchange business has proven to be so profitable that some companies like Trademark Barter Banking of Portland, Oregon, provide such services on a freelance basis.

Taken as a whole, the three-part forms, credit cards, computers, four-color newsletters and "nonbank" banking system are a far cry from the very early forerunners of the trade exchange, the mercantile exchanges of the Middle Ages, and, more recently, the work exchanges that were created all over the United States during the Depression. In *Back to Barter,* Annie Proulx discusses the bank moratorium of March 1933 which led to the creation of hundreds of groups like the Unemployed Citizens' League of Seattle, the Citizens' Service Exchange of Richmond, Virginia, and the National Development Association (NDA) of Salt Lake City.

Work exchanges enabled neighbors to trade goods and services and gave work and hope to millions of the unemployed. At the peak of the work exchange movement, the NDA operated canning factories, an oil refinery, a sawmill, a coal mine and a soap factory, eventually attracting several hundred thousand members in six western states. However, as the country gradually changed over to a war economy and cash business picked up, the exchange idea faded and soon became a quaint but nevertheless frightening reminder of hard times.

Ironically, the exchange idea returned, not in the midst of a depression, but rather during the largest economic boom in U.S. history—the mid-1950s. Melvin Hilton, a Los Angeles toy and cosmetics wholesaler, started the first modern trade exchange, Hilton Exchange, which is still in business more than thirty years later and has served some members for more than two decades.

Hilton remembers, "People would come to my warehouse all the time and offer to trade this or that, but I just wasn't interested. Finally, one day a fellow stopped by wanting to paint my building. He said, 'I have what you want; you have what I want; why can't we trade?' He'd already traded for a yacht and an airplane and had had his buck teeth fixed. He offered to call his dentist for me, and I said, 'Hell, I've already got all the teeth I want.' But he was persistent, and I did it, and then I started to think about trading as an ongoing business."

BUSINESS EXCHANGE

While a cosmetics wholesaler reinvented the trade exchange, it took a billboard salesman and banker named Marvin J. "Mac" McConnell to make the idea work. He was the first trade exchange operator to develop professional accounting systems, the first to franchise and the first to go public. Following his progress from a small local service to a multibranched national entity affords a lesson not only in how to start and run a trade exchange, but also in understanding the problems that come with joining one.

Essentially, styling changes in the automobile put McConnell into the barter business. In the 1950s, operating as Taxineon, Inc., he had been very successfully installing illuminated billboards on the backs of taxi cabs and leasing them to advertisers in 650 cities. In 1954, Studebaker came out with its Champion model, which sloped dramatically in the back. McConnell says, "I could see the handwriting on the wall. If that was the forerunner of what cars were going to look like, I was out of business." That was when he decided to start a small finance company, Inglewood Thrift & Loan, in a Los Angeles suburb and sold off Taxineon city by city; whatever cities and space he couldn't sell, he bartered. He'd already become familiar with that practice in the neon business: "I'd do trade-outs with nightclubs like Ciro's, and hotel scrip and restaurant due bills were always available. I used to say to myself, 'Why doesn't someone create a pool of due bills?' "

One day McConnell remembered the idea while watching his bookkeeper: "I thought, why couldn't pooled due bills function as a credit-and-debit system? After all, banks don't warehouse their inventory. That day, I decided to do it, and I sold the company for seven figures; as it turned out, I needed every penny. I was almost a millionaire and almost a bankrupt in my first four months of bartering."

After several false starts during the late 1950s, he eventually opened the Executive Exchange Club in April 1961. (It later became Business Exchange.) At the time, 600 members paid twenty-five dollars down for annual dues and a one-hundred-dollar initiation fee in installments as well as an all-cash 7 percent transaction fee. Everyone pledged $1,000 in goods or services to the pool and got to pull out $1,000 of somebody else's credits. Therefore, everybody who joined had a $1,000 credit, giving McConnell a pool of due bills worth $600,000.

The business ran like a charm the first month. Trade volume

and commissions were so high—$350,000 and $24,500 respectively—that he quickly opened a second office in San Diego and planned sixteen others. During the second month, business declined slightly; the third month, trading took a big slide and, by the fourth month, there was practically no trading—only $30,000 worth—grossing McConnell a mere $2,100.

Like every other trade exchange operator, McConnell learned quickly and painfully that there are two kinds of barter clients, what he now calls "have" and "have-not" accounts. "Have-not" accounts spent like mad, and, as a result, "have" accounts quickly became loaded with credits, couldn't spend them and stopped trading. In the jargon of the barter industry, "They went on hold" or "on stand-by." In a perfect world, a trade exchange would only sign up "have" clients, whose products and services are in high demand; as things stand, every exchange has both kinds of members.

McConnell also learned that even though barter was conceptually attractive, it couldn't service every business the same way. After some trial and much error, he decided that businesses fell into four basic categories, each of which could use barter in a slightly different way:

1. Professionals, who worked on a 40–50 percent profit margin and could afford to trade their services exclusively for Barter Exchange (BX) credits;

2. Retailers who pay cash for low-priced items and make small profits reselling them—grocery stores and gas stations—who were allowed to buy with 100 percent BX credits and sell on a 50 percent cash, 50 percent trade basis;

3. Big-ticket retailers—sellers of cars, boats, anything over $1,000—who were allowed to negotiate a combination of cash and BX credits with their buyers;

4. Manufacturers and wholesalers, who were also able to negotiate part cash, part BX credit transactions.

Reclassifying businesses and refining his marketing efforts didn't solve another problem: an ironclad accounting system. BX originally issued gold-colored checks which were imprinted with credit limits and had to be cut in half and tallied by hand—a tedious process. His second system used a credit card and a limit on each purchase rather than an overall debt ceiling. The "prepaid credit card" didn't solve the accounting problem nor did a modified credit card and check system, which required purchase approvals twenty-four hours a day, seven days a week.

Finally, just after McConnell had tried his eighth accounting system, he got a call from Eugene Morrow, who had been his operations manager at the bank. Morrow said Inglewood Thrift & Loan was looking for a system to provide supermarkets with a guaranteed system for cashing checks. "The way it worked out, in solving his problem, I solved my own."

The idea was to issue check guarantee stamps, like S&H green stamps, that would be attached to checks and guarantee them up to a certain limit. McConnell explains that, "People still used to save stamps from the previous year and use them the following year to exceed their authorized limit." BX now issues checks to its members and stamps which validate them. Each month, members receive with their statements forty stamps broken into different denominations by a computer. When a member makes a purchase, he writes out a check and validates it with a stamp.

THE GREAT FRANCHISE BOOM—AND BUST

McConnell's success in Los Angeles spawned other trade exchanges, many of which prospered under strong local management and still do. There are currently 300 in business and each averages about $600,000 worth of trades a year, creating commissions worth from $30,000 to $60,000. Some of these businesses are twenty and thirty years old, and they serve their members well. Other franchised exchanges did not. In trying to take the BX concept national by franchising it, McConnell opened a can of worms for business people, many of whom lost hundreds, even thousands of cash dollars when the franchised exchanges they belonged to went out of business. (A California printer wound up with more than 200,000 unspendable trade dollars and estimated that he'd spent $25,000 in labor and supplies to earn them.) In addition, many well-meaning people paid large fees for franchises and watched their investments evaporate due to a total lack of training and support from the franchisor.

Independent trade exchanges work well on the local level because:

- the exchange owner's personal involvement makes transactions happen;
- community considerations obviate the use of cutthroat practices;
- the amount the trade exchange operator and each member invests is relatively small;
- sign-up fees are also small, motivating exchange operators to put extra effort into promoting trades and create cash commissions;
- trade dollars are more spendable, because members can act as their own trade brokers and call around locally to see if certain items are available through trading.

Nationally franchised chains don't work as well because:

- many are owned by out-of-town, even out-of-state, operators;
- there's no community to consider; trade exchanges can and do move frequently;
- operators invest large sums of money to buy franchises, as much as $150,000 in several cases, heightening their expectations and lowering their tolerance to member complaints;
- sign-up fees are sizable, because operators want to recoup their initial investment quickly, making it more desirable economically for them to spend their time signing up new members rather than servicing old ones;
- trade dollars are less spendable, because members are totally

dependent on trade brokers for information on trading opportunities.

Of course, all this is clear only in hindsight. When entrepreneurs heard that McConnell was finding business people eager to
pay $5,000 or more for an exclusive territory in which to operate
a BX franchise, the great barter franchise boom was on. From the
mid-1970s to the early 1980s, it seemed that there was a new
franchised barter operation surfacing every few months.

Unfortunately, these new companies—Mutual Credit Buying (MCB), Unlimited Business Exchange (UBE), International
Trade Exchange (ITE), Exchange Enterprises (EE), Barter Systems, Inc. (BSI)—couldn't supply the advice to match their avarice. No single franchisor came up with a workable plan to help its
franchisee's clients barter profitably. Too much attention was
placed on selling franchises and not nearly enough on training,
supervision and service.

From the public's viewpoint, there was no screening of fran-
chisors. ITE, which grossed $12 million in 1978, mostly in fran-
chise sales, according to *New Ventures* magazine, was started by
Cortes W. Randall, who had served nine months for stock fraud in
connection with the National Student Marketing Corp. scandal.
Secondly, there was no federal policing of barter franchises; the
Securities and Exchange Commission, Federal Trade Commission, Interstate Commerce Commission and the Department of
Commerce under both Republican and Democratic administra-
tions never dealt with national barter abuses. Randall and his
partner, James Dyer, were able to sell forty-six franchises in their
first two years, concentrating their efforts in states that had no
disclosure laws. Lastly, there have never been any controls on the
trade dollar. Many franchises "printed" trade credits with nothing
to back them up; that, in turn, led "have" accounts to become satu-
rated with credits; these "have" accounts subsequently suspend
trading, trading stops, and trade exchanges go out of business.

When a former corporate consultant named Bill Nordstrom
bought the Los Angeles franchise for Barter Systems, I learned
about trade exchanges by publicizing his company for several

years and later publishing a magazine for twelve Barter Systems franchisees. During that time, I traded my services for credits I used to buy office equipment and messenger service, was able to get my wife a pair of diamond earrings, got a Vector Graphics III computer for half cash/half trade, used Continental Airlines tickets for business trips and had a large part of my house tiled and carpeted.

On the other hand, when I needed a bid on painting a set of shutters, I gave one of them to a painter who never returned it despite numerous phone calls. (I found out later he'd moved to New Mexico.) A 1979 Buick, which I'd waited four months to buy, cost me 6,000 trade dollars and needed a complete engine overhaul four months later. Worst of all, I hired an attorney to take care of a collection problem and wound up spending 2,500 trade dollars and $350 in cash costs to settle an unpaid $1,500 publicity bill.

I learned that trade exchanges are an odd mixture of pluses and minuses. On the plus side, they offer an inexpensive way to drum up business, save cash, clear out inventory, expand distribution and increase social contacts in a community. On the minus side, they can consume large amounts of time, can involve overcharges (particularly on services) and, because of greed and incompetence, can leave members holding large amounts of unspendable credits.

Fortunately, many of the most flagrant abuses of trade exchanges are gradually becoming a thing of the past, thanks in large part to the news media, government agencies, a chastened industry association and private enterprise.

Media: The "Gee whiz" tone that accompanied most news articles and broadcast reports about trade exchanges in the 1970s has thankfully given way to a healthier skepticism. Investigative reporters have illuminated the unsavory pasts of people like Randal and Reverend Chuck Wilkerson, who briefly ran Barter Systems while fleeing charges of fraudulent fund-raising in several states. ABC-TV's "20/20" ran a lengthy report on trade exchanges and reported that one member had swapped his house, never got another one in exchange and was in danger of losing everything if the exchange went out of business. Similarly, daily newspapers and business periodicals have done reports on shady trade exchange operators and helped force the worst offenders out of business.

Government: By focusing public attention on possible abuses, the news media have also galvanized local and state government agencies into action against fraudulent exchange operators. In addition to the IRS activities noted earlier, the attorneys general of six states—New York, California, Utah, Texas, Washington and Florida—have ongoing investigations of barter companies. Lastly, the Federal Trade Commission is finally gathering material for the federal government's first investigation into trade exchange abuses.

Industry Groups: The trade exchange industry has had its own trade association since 1979. The International Reciprocal Trade Association (IRTA), originally the International Association of Trade Exchanges (IATE), has absolutely nothing to do with reciprocal trade; nevertheless, when trade exchanges began to attract negative publicity, the organization decided the trade exchange part of its name had to go.

Fortunately, for the public, the cosmetic name change has also been accompanied by a change in leadership and attitude. IATE was formed with the blessings and financial support of Exchange Enterprises and Barter Systems International, two of the most notorious franchised chains, which used it as a device to increase their own respectability. Now, with their principals entirely out of the barter business or under intense local and federal scrutiny, the IRTA has widened its focus beyond trade exchanges to include corporate brokers, media barterers and other barter-related companies.

IRTA did the bread-and-butter lobbying work on TEFRA and contributed to the Barter Self-Regulation Act, which calls for a self-regulating entity like the National Association of Security Dealers (NASD). Just as the NASD operates under statute to the Securities and Exchange Commission, the IRTA would operate under the auspices of the Commerce Department, assuming the bill is passed in its present form.

Private Enterprise: The good intentions of the press, the government and the IRTA would be meaningless without a change of thinking in the private sector. Operating a trade exchange can still be a lucrative way of making a living as the owners of many independent exchanges can attest. While some operators still remain tied to the idea of building a national chain by reviving failed exchanges, one young entrepreneur has a different approach—a well-funded, financially sound franchised chain.

Barter Exchange International (BEI), based in Austin, Texas, is the creation of Matt O'Hayer, who has enlisted the support of the Philadelphia First Group, Inc. (PFG), an investment firm based in a suburb of Philadelphia. John Brown, the firm's executive vice president, was impressed enough with O'Hayer's plan to invest in it and to join BEI's board. He says, "We were attracted by the growth potential and the opportunity to leverage our experience. Our investigation of barter led us to the conclusion that it was a sleazy business in dire need of professionalism, yet could play a significant role in commerce."

Brown's colleague in PFG, Everett Keech, is assistant dean of the Wharton School of Finance and chairs BEI's board of directors. Moreover, he's no newcomer to barter. While serving as Assistant Secretary of the Air Force in 1976–77, Keech got firsthand experience in countertrade (international barter); he administered a deal under which Northrop and General Electric had contracted to sell more than $200 million worth of Swiss goods as part of a $500 million sale of F-5 fighter planes to Switzerland. (See Chapter 9.)

About BEI, Keech says, "I like this little company. I think it's the wave of the future, even though it's misnamed; we don't barter, and we're not an exchange. We're a third-party record-keeper with slick computers and stringent credit checks. We're a service bureau; we operate the system, keep score and sign up the players."

His goal is attracting 10,000 clients. "When we reach that, once we provide the widest possible range of goods and services, we're dealing in ultimate liquidity—a new kind of currency." Yet financial success alone won't be enough for Keech. "Barter is going to have to be perceived as clean. It must be policed and regulated with enforcement from something like the NASD (National Association of Security Dealers). Right now, trade exchanges are where securities were in 1931; everybody is either a crook or is perceived as being a crook."

BEI started operating in February 1983, and there are currently thirty offices which add their city name and operate as Houston Barter Exchange, Louisville Barter Exchange, etc. PFG raised $500,000 for the company in November, 1983, supplies business and financial advice, and provides a bold contrast to the unprofessional approach of most trade exchange franchisors and franchisees. O'Hayer says, "The vast majority of them don't know what a financial statement is. And, when you talk about a Big Eight group, they think of Nebraska's football team, not Peat, Marwick & Mitchell."

He sees this lack of financial background as the first reason most trade exchanges fail. "Most operators start by purchasing products from their first clients and liquidating it; they rob the system and put nothing back." The second is that, "the other chains teach their franchisees to start a trade exchange without enough cash. They make a franchisee think, 'Hey, I can have my very own money tree, and, anytime I feel like it, I can loan myself all the money I want.' It does work that way for a short period of time, but then everyone winds up with big trade balances, and trading stops. They have to understand they're running an economy, just like the President."

While Business Exchange clients can also trade on either a 100 percent trade basis or a 50 percent cash–50 percent trade basis, Barter Exchange clients can sell on a half-trade, half-cash basis and buy on a 100 percent trade basis by maintaining a balance of 5,000 trade dollars. BEI clients can also buy on time and get loans with trade dollars. "We operate like a finance company. If you have a zero balance and want to deficit spend, you can go to our credit department, and they'll work out a loan just like a bank would."

Franchisees are screened thoroughly, and, O'Hayer adds proudly, BEI ends every business day with a zero trade dollar balance as mandated by the company's bylaws. In other words, every BEI credit issued is offset by a debit and each credit is backed by some tangible form of collateral. He tried unsuccessfully to get the IRTA to adopt zero balances as an industry standard but has since joined IRTA's board and is trying to change the system from within. He's upbeat about that organization, the future of barter and his own company. "We already have our bread-and-butter business, and we were profitable from our first quarter."

O'Hayer's optimism is shared by Bob Meyer, the former Milwaukee Brewer relief pitcher, who publishes *Barter News*. Meyer predicts, "Even with the problems, the trade exchange has a great future as a business, because there's a real need for it at the local level." Meyer also thinks strong local independent exchanges will reassert themselves again. "When every other word you heard was BSI, BX, EE, these guys got lost in the shuffle; people like Fred Detwiler in Detroit, Gary Cooper in Charlotte, and Mike Ames in Orange County has always run clean operations, and they're going to be the leaders again."

SEVEN POINTS TO KEEP IN MIND

The future of strong, locally run trade exchanges does seem brighter with the demise of the franchised trade exchange as originally conceived. While it remains to be seen if Barter Exchange's plan can work on a national level, a more aware public, a heightened governmental role and a real possibility of self-regulation signal perhaps that, despite its checkered past, the trade exchange business has a bright future. If you're investigating a trade exchange, you should keep these points in mind:

1. Check it out. Before you become a member of a trade exchange, ask for a bank reference; see if your Better Business Bureau or District Attorney has had any complaints from other members of the exchange. Call the IRTA (202-537-1446) and ask if the exchange is a member. Ask your attorney, banker, accountant and other business associates for any information they may have.

2. Negotiate a trial membership. You have more bargaining power as a prospective member than you do after actually signing up. If you're considering joining an exchange, consider that it would rather have a provisional new member than no new member at all.

3. Negotiate a performance clause. Most business contracts specify various levels of achievement for both parties. Give the exchange a specified period of time to deliver on their promises.

4. Maintain multiple relationships. If you do decide to join, make sure you develop relationships with several people in the exchange; if you only talk to one person and he or she leaves, you'll have to start again. The company only wants you to deal with one person because it's more cost effective from their viewpoint, but that's not the way to make the most of your membership. Also, make a point of stopping by every once in a while. Your face has more impact than a phone call.

5. Be specific. If you're trading for services, make sure the person providing them knows exactly what you need in advance; this attitude guards against honest misunderstandings as well as jacked-up estimates. If you're unloading an inventory and you want to make sure these products don't show up at cut-rate prices in your usual sales outlets, write—and make sure the trade exchange signs—a separate letter of agreement covering that inventory.

6. Remember that trade dollars are dollars. Some trade exchange members get frustrated by their inability to get exactly what they want on trade and, as a consequence, they spend credits wildly. Even though they're trade dollars, they become real dollars on April 15 and are taxable as income so don't waste them, particularly on nondeductible personal items.

7. Don't trade more than you can afford. Trade exchange membership can be very seductive; make sure it remains a mere adjunct to your cash business. U.S. Steel sets a limit on how many credits it will absorb; you too should set a limit for your own trading activities and stick with it.

While trade exchanges offer an excellent means of bartering for professionals and small businesses, large corporations require a fundamentally different approach, because they are national, even international entities. To meet their specific needs, companies have sprung up that promise coast-to-coast service, greater attention to detail and more protection from financial risk; they're called corporate brokers.

CHAPTER 7

CORPORATE BROKERS AND SEQUENTIAL TRADERS

As more and more major corporations became involved with trade exchanges, some became disenchanted and started searching for alternative ways to accomplish the same goals—conserving cash, disposing of inventory, finding new customers—through a different method of bartering.

Some, like 3M, Avis and Republic Airlines, started in-house bartering operations and were successful at it; others used established barter firms with track records of serving major corporate clients—firms like Deerfield Communications, which has worked with General Motors and National Semiconductor, and Atwood Richards, which has represented U.S. Steel and Liggett & Myers.

These corporate brokers are like trade exchanges only in that they perform the clearinghouse function, operate by trading overproduced items which can't be sold for cash profitably, accept goods and services and issue barter credits against them. Corporate brokers have no interest in banking, they don't issue credit cards and three-part forms, and they don't make loans and don't pay interest.

Instead, they use the receivables deal model explained earlier (page 39) and take in their clients' goods and services; then they repay those clients partly by issuing credits and partly in cash from the liquidation of goods and services. Credit balances are reduced whenever cash or goods are received. Due to the nature of their business, companies like these face greater risks than trade exchanges. First, they don't have sure sources of income like membership fees and generate income only when they actually make deals. Secondly, their risk is higher because they usually assume legal ownership of the goods rather than simply act as a middleman.

Despite these risks, several trade exchange franchisees, a travel barterer and a stock manipulator have tried to combine the best elements of both corporate brokerages and trade exchanges; all three attempts have been less than totally successful. Four Barter Systems franchisees declared their franchise agreements illegal and formed the short-lived TradeGroup, Ltd. which signed up only one major client, Scott Paper Co., before collapsing as a result of inadequate funding.

The travel barterer, Phillip Stein, had traded hotel rooms and airline seats for fourteen years through his own company, Convention Group Specialists, but saw the need for a trade exchange that would service major corporations exclusively and make money by charging large initiation and annual membership fees and taking a 6 percent cash commission from the buyer. He was able to get the cooperation of William Spencer, former president of Citicorp, Jack Parker, former vice chairman of General Electric, and, eventually, superbanker Walter Wriston. With their financial expertise and contacts, he was able to sign up more than fifty major corporations including Du Pont, Hertz, Travelers Insurance and Gannett.

A typical Univex deal involved United Technologies (UT), Holiday Inn, Trans World Airlines (TWA) and *Playboy*. *Playboy* had originally considered buying an $850,000 telephone system from Rolm Corp., but, upon joining Univex, discovered it could get an equivalent system from UT in exchange for ad space. (Since UT would not have gotten the business without bartering, this transaction is a good example of using barter as a marketing advantage.) UT used its $799,000 worth of credits ($850,000 minus Univex's six percent commission) to purchase TWA airline tickets and hotel rooms from Holiday Inns, and *Playboy* sold ad space to other Univex clients to pay for the phone system.

Yet such deals have proven infrequent, and Univex had not shown a profit in its first three years of operations. Moreover, the company's focus has shifted away from bartering, and Stein denies Univex is involved in bartering at all. He insists vehemently that "it's a *trading* company. Bartering is not good for anyone but the barterers. It alienates ad agencies, dealers and distributors." Stein maintains, "The Univex method doesn't demean the reputation of *Fortune* 500 companies. Bartering is a thing of the past; there isn't one barterer that's made money."

Neither did Univex, which showed a deficit of $2.1 million during its start-up phase. Now, the corporate strategy has changed, and Univex is trying to serve its clients in three new ways. It has (1) consolidated their purchasing power to buy everyday business items in bulk; (2) advised them about purchasing opportunities offered by qualified minority suppliers; and (3) created a joint venture with Tendler, Beretz & Associates to service some of their needs in countertrade. (David Tendler and Hal Beretz were, respectively, the CEO and president of Phibro/Salomon Brothers, the international trading company.) Along with its new business plan, Univex has a new CEO, Jim Collins, who formerly headed Red Devil Paints, and has raised another $2.5 million in private financing.

The third entrepreneur who tried to mate the trade exchange concept with a corporate clientele is Bob Goldsamt, a former investment banker, who founded three other public companies in the health field before beginning Integrated Barter International (IBI). In 1976, Goldsamt tried to sell 3,000 cash memberships to a racquetball club in Aspen, Colorado, and, when business was slow, joined a local trade exchange. The exchange sold several hundred memberships for him but then went bankrupt, sticking Goldsamt with thousands of unspendable credits.

Despite this unfortunate introduction, Goldsamt became interested in barter, and originally flirted with the idea of starting a national trade exchange by buying reputable independent exchanges in various parts of the country and then consolidating them; after buying exchanges in Pittsburgh and Long Island, however, he realized they were essentially local entities and changed his focus. He resold the exchanges and decided to combine existing barter companies in several different categories: (1) companies that buy media, airline tickets, hotel rooms, etc. on a barter basis; (2) sequential traders like Atwood Richards, which make money by acquiring products and services and retrading them (see below); and (3) cash converters, which trade for products and services, then convert them back into cash.

He met America's best-known liquidator, Sam Nassi, at a time when Nassi had begun liquidating inventories in partnership with Deerfield. Working together, the two bought National Semiconductor's inventories of calculators and watches for $10.5 million and Mattel's $11.8 million inventory of hand-held electronic games, providing media, meeting rooms and products in return. Seeing these companies as the core of a barter-based distribution company, Goldsamt bought them in 1983, along with International Asset Management (a countertrade specialist) and F&F Merchandising (a toy and game liquidator) for $23 million. Since then, IBI has also added a media-buying company and a reseller of brand name men's wear and also started joint ventures with a direct marketing company and an appraiser.

While Univex provides the clearinghouse and collects commissions like a trade exchange, IBI was designed to be a purchasing and distribution company that takes in products and services from companies such as GTE and Nike and issues barter credits against them, just as in the receivables deals outlined earlier. A separate fulfillment division works to spend these credits on goods and services for which the corporations ordinarily would have paid cash.

Like Univex, IBI pools the purchasing power of its clients and buys things that every business can use—shipping containers, office supplies, etc. While Nike and Mattel can get very good prices on their own, pooled together with other IBI clients, they can get even a better one.

As in the receivables deal outlined in Chapter 4, IBI:

1. issues credits against inventories of products and services;
2. pools its clients' purchasing power;
3. computes the difference between the pooled price and the

price a company would ordinarily have paid for a given
item when it makes a deal;

4. applies that difference against credits assigned to clients
in exchange for their inventories, along with a percentage
of the cash it gets upon liquidation.

F&F bought an estimated 500,000 cradle phones from General Telephone & Electronics; Deerfield offered them to hotels,
and IBI's direct marketing arm used them to sign up new sub-
scribers to various magazines and is also selling them as a "per
inquiry" (PI) item on TV. Every time a viewer calls to request
more information (an inquiry), the TV station is paid a set fee or a
percentage of the sales price for generating this sales lead. Similarly, when Deerfield signed a multi-million dollar deal with a
sportswear maker, Nassi handled distribution of the goods and
IBI's media buyers bought magazine space and TV time for the
manufacturer.

Unfortunately, this multi-ring circus began running into cash
flow problems toward the end of 1985. Rather than continue to
pay a salary to Nassi, IBI sought to accrue it until his division
turned a profit; Nassi refused to go along, and the two began a
legal battle. In view of the situation, company auditors decided
that the full purchase price of Nassi's company—$10.4 mil-
lion—had to be written off completely. The resulting domino effect caused IBI's stock to plummet from seven dollars a share to
thirty-seven cents, and another public issue of $8 million was re-
scinded by the Securities and Exchange Commission.

SEQUENTIAL TRADING: BARTER LEVERAGE

While these efforts to serve large corporations in trade exchange
fashion have had their problems, a different kind of corporate
brokerage firm has been largely successful in helping large corporations barter their inventories. Such companies, known as
"sequential traders," originally buy or trade for a given inventory
and keep on retrading it for commodities worth larger and larger

dollar amounts until they've significantly increased their initial investment.

We've already seen that, on the simplest level, barter possesses an inherent capacity for leverage; it stretches purchasing power by allowing companies and professionals to "sell" at retail and "buy" at wholesale. It can also offer financial leverage when goods and services are translated into equity, bad debts are transformed into performing assets, and inventory is converted into a tax deduction or write-off.

Sequential trading takes full advantage of a different kind of leverage which is based on the reasonable assumption that business people would rather get some return on their investment than none. Consider the position of manufacturers of seasonal items (Easter egg dye, snowmobiles), marketers of fashion items (records, clothing, posters) and media and travel companies (broadcasters, hotels and airlines). They can't take the chance that their excess capacity will go totally unsold; accordingly, they trade away that uncertainty. They transform their excess inventory into credits, then use the credits to buy needed materials.

Let's say your company makes small household appliances, and you're stuck with an inventory of popcorn poppers. If a barter company traded them for radio time which you could then use to promote another product (say your electric can openers), you'd be thrilled. You wouldn't know—or care—that the company was using your popcorn poppers as the opening gambit in a complicated eight-way trade. On the other hand, if you were infused with entrepreneurial spirit, you might take the poppers and make a deal with a broadcaster yourself, trying to negotiate three dollars' worth of radio time for every dollar's worth of poppers, then keep increasing its value by retrading it again and again and again.

That's what sequential traders do; they start with cash, products or services and keep making deal after deal after deal, taking perhaps as many as eight separate steps before "The Game" ends. Ed Hartnett, executive vice president of Media General Broadcast Services, a leading media trader, explains that "A true barterer doesn't have any easy deals; the more complicated the deal, the greater the satisfaction."

The financial satisfaction can be considerable when sequential deals work; there are examples of barter companies eventually getting five, ten, even twenty times the return on their initial investment; when they don't work . . . well, that's why there are only a handful of sequential traders in the U.S.

Like everything else, barter leverage has its price. In this case, the price consists of using a lot of time and energy locating and negotiating each element of the trade, taking title to goods and usually paying to warehouse them until they're resold. Obviously, this imposes greater risks than the average corporate broker is used to—spoilage, spillage, breakage, acts of God, labor disputes, political unrest, etc. It also requires more initial capital and a need for absolute precision. Like tightrope walkers, sequential traders can't afford many false steps.

That's why most sequential traders are, literally, world-class traders. Moreton Binn of Atwood Richards traded steel for the Eiffel Tower restaurant and subsequently retraded it (at a profit) to a New Orleans restaurateur; Deerfield's Fred Tarter once took a boatload of damaged bananas from South America and was able to trade them to a baby food company in the Midwest for machinery.

Similarly, Roger Davis, founder of the Countertrade Roundtable of New York, created a $1.6 million five-way swap which started and ended in the Midwest but required eleven months and 46,000 air miles to complete. In 1983, he exchanged U.S. construction equipment for Venezuelan oil, sent the oil to Czechoslovakia for shoe-making machinery, swapped the machinery in Argentina for animal hides, exchanged the hides for frozen orange juice in Brazil, and finally sold the juice to a Midwestern grocery chain.

Such Milo Minderbinder machinations are now possible because computers and telecommunications are making international sequential trading less risky. Two men who formerly ran in-house trading departments for large conservative corporations have just become sequential traders—Dennis Needham, who ran Republic Airlines' unit, and Bob Morgan, who headed 3M's Corporate Trade Center.

Morgan bought the name from 3M and just started Corporate Trade Center in Minneapolis. Now 3M is his client rather than his employer, and he also represents Yamaha and other large manufacturers. Trading 3M products like tape recorders and billboard space taught him that sequential trading had a lot to recommend it as opposed to other bartering methods like working through trade exchanges. He says, "Basically, trade exchanges take your goods and give you promissory notes. If they deliver, everybody's happy. If they don't, there are lots of problems. Their biggest problem is they don't understand how to run their business so that everybody wins. There's plenty of room for everyone to make a profit—if they don't get greedy."

Morgan will take an inventory on consignment and typically trade it for broadcasting time—at a leveraged ratio in his favor. "Broadcasters always need merchandise for promotions and they have time that has no value if it goes unsold, so they're an obvious outlet." He'll generally trade in three or four steps and eventually cash out, or, alternatively, he'll simply trade an inventory and take a fee. "I don't take title unless I'm sure I can move the goods; however, if you do it right, this can be a wonderful business. It's low-risk, there's almost no capital investment and the return on investment approaches infinity."

Dennis Needham and Chris Todd, the president of Commonwealth Trading, Inc. (also in Minneapolis), buy full or partial inventories, then try to leverage them before cashing out. They recently bought footwear which, contractually, had to be sold outside the U.S., then traded it for African frozen fish, which they had prearranged to sell for cash at a large profit. In another instance, they took products from a company that owed CBS-TV money for satellite transponder time, traded the products for electronic goods and converted them into airline tickets that CBS used to cover golf tournament expenses; thus, CBS was paid money it was owed, and Commonwealth made another healthy profit.

From the client's standpoint, there really is very little difference between working with a corporate broker and with a sequential trader. Corporate brokers probably offer greater security and discretion, plus they have greater entree to bankers and financiers which may be necessary on large deals. On the other hand, sequential traders probably offer quicker results. Before they agree to take your inventory, they'll have already figured out its next destination, leading to a faster payback for you, particularly on part-cash, part-trade deals.

While corporate brokers trade inventories all at once, make a fee and go on to the next deal, Todd and other sequential traders may be perceived as always being in the middle of one endless, ongoing deal. If any single person symbolizes this wheeler-dealer mentality it is Moreton Binn, the self-styled "Baron of Barter."

Binn, who served his business apprenticeship in sales promotion, got the barter bug while working for a breakfast cereal client. While promoting the cereal with a contest that offered trips to Europe, he learned that he could get free airline tickets by mentioning the airline's name prominently in ads supporting the promotion. From that vantage point, it was easy to take the next step and build a business to leverage airline tickets, media time and other commodities.

He bought Atwood Richards specifically because the company had traded extensively with broadcasters. Instead of trading for broadcasting clients and constantly having to find ways to keep them happy, he began trading for himself which made sense for everyone. Promotion managers only cared about divesting their potentially unused time for usable products or services which Binn was able to deliver in most cases. Having satisfied them in the first step of a trade, he was able to go through five or six others, increasing his leverage every step of the way. In one typical case, he:

1. laid out $100,000 in cash to buy a high-ticket amplifier for a large cash-pressed radio station which was low on cash and got $200,000 worth of air time in return;
2. swapped the air time for $250,000 worth of golf clubs

which he actually bought for $215,500 owing to the size of the deal;

3. exchanged the clubs for $375,000 worth of hotel rooms and services at a major resort; and
4. traded the hotel rooms to a CB radio manufacturer for $63,750 in cash and $311,250 in radios.

When all these machinations were through, he had recovered nearly two thirds of his cash investment, and he *still* had $311,250 worth of CB radios to play with. In essence, he had taken $36,250 and bought $311,250 worth of merchandise with it, a better than eight-to-one ratio.

Such leveraging legerdemain is second nature to Binn, who says, "Everyone I talk to goes through three separate reactions. First, they don't understand barter, at least not the way we do it. Then they can't understand that we make money at it. Finally, when they *do* begin to understand, they're appalled at the money we make."

Others are merely appalled at his demands. When Italy's oldest families asked him to develop tourist business for San Marino, *Newsweek* reported that Binn demanded "a chunk of the country." Yet, similar *chutzpah* led him to arrange a floating sales meeting for Parker Pen aboard the *Queen Elizabeth II* (as part of a trade that indirectly involved millions of dollars' worth of pens) and also make what business columnist Dan Dorfman called "a very realistic offer" to buy Chrysler Corporation's unsold 1979 inventory before the government bail-out (of which more later).

Chrysler had a problem as do all businesses that talk with Binn, a man who makes his living by trading other people's mistakes. "The thing that makes this business go is that no one operates at 100 percent efficiency, and no one produces exactly the right product in exactly the right quantity." *Marketing*, a British advertising magazine, put it this way: "Moreton Binn would be about as welcome at a new product launch as an undertaker in a maternity ward." Binn agrees. "Every time a new product comes on the market, somebody gets stuck with the old model. The manufacturer can still sell yesterday's item, but he has to cut prices—and profits—to do it. But, if he gives it to us, he gets rid of his inventory and improves his cash flow at the same time; we're the ideal elephants' graveyard."

Touring Binn's graveyard, the fifteenth floor of 99 Park Avenue in New York City, is like entering a marketing "Believe It or Not." You find yourself asking, "Someone actually tried to market instant cheese-flavored grits? Monster Multiple Vitamins? Leroy Neiman Commemorative Whiskey Bottles?" If these seem improbable, consider that, on a typical day, a *partial* list of Atwood's inventory (whether stored in his clients' warehouses or his own) included:

301	grandfather's clocks
15	Lotus sports cars
1,960	lawnmowers
8,900	cases of designer chocolates
13,000	record turntables
520	telex machines
73	combines
786	collapsible portable bicycles
2,205	log splitters
592	Swiss watches
80,000	hydroponic houseplants

as well as $2.25 million worth of industrial conveyor belting, $2 million worth of refractory brick, $500,000 worth of airfreight service, resort hotel space, rental cars, customs brokerage services, and baseball tickets.

To keep track, Binn has two full-time secretaries to go with his two limousines—a Rolls-Royce and a Cadillac—each of which has, naturally, two telephones. Short, stocky and just beginning to lose a little hair at forty-seven, he likens bartering to being a floor trader on the New York Stock Exchange. He says, with a boyish glint, "I like it. It keeps me awake."

It's been keeping him awake since October 31, 1974, when he and several other investors, whom he later bought out, purchased Atwood. From the outset, Binn concentrated on two facts of business life: (1) expenditures continue while merchandise sits in warehouses and (2) everything can be sold for a price. "You don't need to be a genius to sell something at ten cents on the dollar. At the right price, anything sells."

Naturally, his clients are insistent about receiving the best possible price for their goods. Binn meets that price by issuing them credits usually good for two or three years, turning their inventory into a receivable; then they can use the credits to buy other products and services he will either trade for or already has in his own sizable inventory.

One satisfied customer is Bob Conley, director of purchasing at U.S. Steel. He supervises all the company's reciprocal trades and also co-manages its four-year-old relationship with Atwood Richards along with Bill Hughes, one of the company's general managers of sales; Hughes is, in essence, the seller, and Conley the buyer in dealings with Atwood. They work together and consult constantly "to keep things in balance."

Conley says most corporations barter for purchasing-related reasons, which he considers the wrong reasons. "Barter companies bring no expertise to the purchasing end of our business. They don't know the market or the prices like an informed buyer. Secondly, money has a time value; you lose some of it if you don't turn it over quickly. If you have a constant balance of $1 million in trade credits, it's costing you $100,000 a year [in unearned interest] not to spend it." He adds, however, that the headaches are worth it if barter results in new business. "We thought bartering would open new markets for us and might produce sales we couldn't make any other way; we took products we use in our day-to-day operations, and we work with a set amount of credits up to an absolute dollar limit. We've made a rational decision to barter for sales penetration, which has had long-range benefits for the company."

Binn makes sure that such clients remain satisfied by meeting the many restrictions they impose on the reselling of their inventory. These conditions come generally in the form of "buts." "We want you to dispose of our products, BUT not in the United

States." Or, "We need to move these goods, BUT we don't want to antagonize our dealer network." Or, ultimately, "Please take this stuff off our hands, BUT don't break the price."

Once, Binn accepted hundreds of Leica cameras with variations of all three restrictions simultaneously:

1. The retail price of $1,000 per camera could not be discounted under any circumstances;
2. Atwood had to use a new alternate method of distribution—i.e., other than camera shops;
3. No matter how Atwood solved the problem, Leica's prestige image had to be reinforced.

On his way to lunch one day, Binn passed a neighborhood bank, went inside and asked a few questions. Three weeks later, full-page ads began running in *The New York Times* offering a $1,000 Leica camera to anyone opening up a money market account at that bank for $10,000. Not only did Binn meet all of Leica's conditions; he also gave them a bonus in the form of prestige newspaper advertising that was beyond the reach of their normal ad budget.

One of the most common restrictions clients request is secrecy, and Binn readily agrees to it, but sometimes regrets it. Pat Ross, president of B. F. Goodrich, was lecturing about creativity in buying, and Binn remembers, "Never once did he mention barter. After the session, I went up to him and said, 'Pat, you're one of our biggest clients. Why didn't you bring up barter as a way of being creative in your purchasing?' He told me, 'I look on barter as a competitive edge, and I don't want anyone to know I do it.' "

Not unnaturally, secrecy about the relationship led to an embarrassing corporate snafu at Goodrich. Binn says, "There was a plant in Ohio which the owners had been trying to unload, unsuccessfully, for a year and half. We were able to offer them products they would normally have paid cash for. They didn't know it, but we were really buying the building for Goodrich. Unfortunately—and obviously without our knowledge—Goodrich was bidding against us. Even worse, they paid $4.5 million in cash when we'd made a deal for $6 million in credits!"

If Binn has discovered that secrecy sometimes causes problems for his clients, he's learned the hard way that publicity can cause problems for himself. In December 1979, Binn had offered to buy Chrysler's Corporation's year-end inventory—5,000 cars and 7,000 trucks—for a combination of $4,000 cash and $2,800 in credits per vehicle, or $81.6 million. To make the deal even sweeter, he'd prearranged for Chrysler to use the credits to buy needed tires and upholstery. Finally, Atwood would transfer the cash part of the deal, $48 million, to Chrysler immediately—no terms, no conditions, no waiting for the money.

Instead, shortly thereafter, Chrysler announced a six-day $2,000 cash discount. Tipped off by one of Binn's associates, Dan Dorfman did a column on the nondeal and reported, "A [Chrysler] spokesman . . . acknowledged that the incentives could cost the company about $24 million in discounts, but he said, 'Getting them out of the inventory is cheaper for us than keeping them.' " Dorfman then asked, "Why would the automaker—so desperate for cash—take a $4,500 cash offer from its dealers payable in roughly twenty to thirty days (the time it would take them to raise the financing) instead of a $4,000 cash offer payable immediately? And for that $500 difference, it's tossing away a credit of $2,500 per unit. In essence it's forfeiting a thirty-day cash flow (the use of Atwood's money) . . . as well as blowing $20 million."

Unable to conceal his outrage, Binn was quoted by Dorfman as saying, "I can't believe it. These guys have to be real jerks. No wonder they may go down the tubes." Chrysler spokesmen made equally insulting remarks in rebuttal, and both parties came off looking a good deal less than their best. (Binn later tried to make amends with a sizable donation to Lee Iacocca's favorite charity, but the offer was politely declined.)

That one got away, but Binn has worked for years with clients like Pepperidge Farm, Schick, and Rolls-Royce, and grosses nine figures a year wheeling and dealing. Nevertheless, he laments the fact that most *Fortune* 500 companies aren't run by free-swinging marketeers like himself. "Economists, not marketing men, are running companies these days. They bring in a new ad manager, give him less money to spend and tell him to clear out the warehouse and increase sales next year."

On the other hand, Binn shrewdly recognizes that a bottom-line orientation can only mean more business for him. "That same ad manager, he has to learn to be creative, to stretch his budget; that's where barter comes in. Manufacturing is a guessing game; our business never goes bad, because somebody always guesses wrong."

SIX REMINDERS FOR CORPORATE CLIENTS

Working with corporate brokers and sequential traders that flash impressive lists of satisfied big-name clients can be economically rewarding and informative; it can also create new headaches to replace the old ones. To make sure that you get the best deal possible:

1. Weigh other alternatives. The pluses in working with a Univex or an Atwood Richards are size and speed; the minus is possibly not being able to spend credits on anything worthwhile. If you happen to represent a sizable company, you may be able to cut a more favorable one-shot deal with a national trade exchange. If you've got a fairly high-priced item, perhaps it can be disposed of in the premium and incentive field. If you're thinking of working with a sequential trader, a reciproal deal may accomplish the same kind of non-competitive distribution you're after with less risk involved.

2. Protect your investment. A well-drawn contract is the key to making sure you receive an adequate return on your inventory. That means creating one that's precise and enforceable with specific performance clauses and penalties for nonperformance. (It also means getting your lawyers to give full consideration to every element and not to be merely a rubber stamp.) If the bartering company insists on their "standard" contract, think hard and long about exploring other alternatives. There is *no* "standard deal" in barter.

3. Start small. Pilot programs are sensible anyway, but here they protect against major disappointments (and corporate embarrassments); moreover, they can offer a low-risk guide to what you can realistically expect in the way of compensation. Instead of two years, try to negotiate a three-month deal with the goods reverting to you if the credits can't be used to your satisfaction.

4. Alert your staff to the deal. Rather than sticking your head in the sand and hoping for the best, write your regional and branch offices and tell them what you're doing. First, you can avoid the type of mix-up in which B. F. Goodrich became involved. Second, if some of your merchandise should start showing up locally, in violation of the contract, your staff will let you know about it as soon as it happens.

5. Set a trading limit. If reciprocal deals and trade exchange transactions are fun, working with corporate brokers and sequential traders can be positively exhilarating; however, you have to lash yourself to the mast and remain practical about the place trading has in your game plan. Don't get carried away by the colored lights and forget your cash customers. Trading is fun, but cash pays the light bill. Set an absolute dollar limit on your trading activity and stick with it.

6. Divide responsibilities. Follow U.S. Steel's excellent example and have two different people working with your barter company, one selling, one buying. By separating their functions but combining their information, you'll get maximum mileage out of your barter company.

7. Be realistic. Many corporate brokers promise the moon in hopes of making a deal and worry about the fulfillment of the bargain later. True, you're currently stuck with an inventory that you want to dispose of quickly and easily, but when a salesman tells you wonderful things he can do for you that seem outlandish, an alarm should go off in your head. Look behind the easy promises for some measure of performance by checking with previous clients.

Most of the companies covered in this chapter, particularly

the sequential traders, often use advertising time and space, airplane tickets and hotel rooms as a means to an end; other companies specialize in providing precisely these commodities on a barter basis. It's time to meet these masters of time and space—the travel and media specialists.

CHAPTER 8

MEDIA AND TRAVEL

A friend of mine is working with Neil Diamond's manager and trying to get him to do concerts on cruise ships. Talent is a lot like travel; you can't pin down what it's worth, which makes it the perfect thing to trade.
—Travel trader DAVE WAGENVOORD

Advertising agencies take you across the country in a Cadillac; we'll get you to the same place in a Buick or an Oldsmobile.
—TOM TANSKI, President, *Broadcast Marketing, Inc.*

Advertising and travel have a lot in common where the average small business is concerned. Both are expensive and, while they may produce more customers, both are really luxuries. On the other hand, both are also very competitive fields and, as such, are subject to seasonal slowdowns, generally in the winter and summer. As highly desirable commodities that inevitably involve excess inventory—unsold broadcasting time and magazine and newspaper space, unfilled hotel rooms and airline seats—they are perfect fodder for barter.

We've already seen how corporate brokers and sequential traders take advertising time and space and increase their value through trading. These trades generally involve three parties—the client, the broker and the broadcaster; however, when media or travel barter specialists are involved, barter transactions often become a four-handed game, because an advertising agency may also be involved—often reluctantly.

The reason for this reticence is that ad agencies have a long-standing love-hate relationship with barter. They love barter syndication, a cashless method of distributing radio and television programming over which they exercise total control, but they dislike all other combinations of broadcasting and bartering or travel and trading. Ad agencies with travel clients are, as a rule, almost forced to accept part of their fees in tickets or scrip; in addition, they often lose commissions when their clients buy media through barter companies.

On the other hand, barter syndication is, despite its name, a cash business from the agency point of view. In this form of distribution, a radio or TV station receives free programming in exchange for airing national commercials packaged with it; recently, it's become a $600 million business. Such successful shows as "Entertainment Tonight," "Fame," and "Solid Gold" would not have been feasible without barter syndication. "Fame" was canceled by NBC in 1983, but Metro Goldwyn Mayer/United Artists and LBS Communications were able to keep it on the air by obtaining upfront money for production from advertisers and selling the show on a barter syndication basis.

Barter syndication has grown rapidly ($30 million in the mid-1970s to $600 million in 1985) because it echoes barter's inherent logic and solves problems for the producer, the advertiser, the agency and the station. The producer gets a show on the air that might otherwise go begging; the advertiser hits precisely the audience its research shows is the demographic target and is also assured that the commercials will run. (In point of fact, other forms of broadcast barter work on an "as available" basis, which means cash customers regularly "bump" bartered spots.) The agency makes a commission it may continue to earn long after its work on the show is finished. The station gets professionally produced programming free and barters time that might otherwise go unsold anyway. As a bonus, it also gets to sell local commercials within the show. (A bartered hour-long radio or TV show may actually be only fifty-four minutes long, leaving room for twelve thirty-second local commercials to be sold by the station.)

I got to see the process firsthand while doing publicity for several radio production companies involved in barter, including one now-defunct firm called the PH Factor. When Warner-Lambert Co., the chemical giant, decided to market Chewels gum, its ad agency, Ted Bates & Co., approached the PH Factor about creating and producing a radio show that would hit teenaged girls (ages twelve to eighteen)—Warner-Lambert's target audience. The PH Factor came up with a sixty-second featurette called "Just a Minute," which included an interview with a well-known rock star and several mentions of Chewels; it eventually aired six times daily in precisely those markets (geographically separate, but demographically similar) where Warner-Lambert had arranged for distribution of the gum.

While most small businesses can't fund national projects on this level, they can often finance regional versions. Let's say, for instance, that a midwestern soft drink manufacturer wanted to test market its brand in the East as a first step toward national distribution. The marketing department and ad agency have picked Connecticut as a likely test market site and have also settled on radio as the most effective advertising medium to reach a young audience. Going the cash route and buying time on dozens of small stations might prove to be expensive and might not make much impact for an unfamiliar soda in a field that's very brand-name conscious.

Instead, through its ad agency, the company could approach stations in the four or five largest cities and offer exclusive live coverage of the Connecticut high school basketball championships on a barter syndication basis from the opening round to the finals. Like Warner-Lambert, the soda-maker would be offering a noncontroversial quality product with strong local identification; one which the station might have carried anyway, if it had had the idea, and one which might produce good community relations and publicity benefits for the station.

Ideas like this one have made barter syndication a separate media-buying category at most major agencies and the fastest-growing part of broadcasting by dollar volume. It also has a euphemistic new name—advertiser-supported television—its own trade association, the Advertiser Supported Television Association, and new respectability.

Things have gotten to the point where CBS, formerly "the most aggressive network in bad-mouthing barter," according to *Advertising Age*, has just launched its *own* international barter TV division. Under a recent agreement, the People's Republic of China will select sixty-five hours of programming it wants *without paying for it*—shows like "Sixty Minutes" and NCAA basketball—and CBS will then sell the time to sponsors; however, CBS denies it's in the barter business. CBS senior vice president John Eger told *Electronic Media*, "We don't call it a barter arrangement . . . that has a lot of connotations. We call it a sponsorship program arrangement."

Eger used the euphemism to avoid putting CBS and barter syndication in the same context because a barter syndication scandal had recently rocked the advertising world. On February 16, 1982, J. Walter Thompson, the nation's largest publicly owned advertising agency, announced it was writing off $18 million of nonexistent income which had been "falsely inflated through fictitious accounting entries" on the books of its barter syndication unit; by April 5, the final total had reached $30 million. This shortfall was discovered accidentally when the 1981 recession slowed collections, and a new financial team went hunting for cash. They discovered, quite unexpectedly, that the barter syndication unit had no revenues whatsoever. Further investigation revealed that someone with access to the unit's computer had boosted revenues artificially by recording entries for programs that had never run and adding commercial time that had never been resold to clients. Thompson changed the mechanics of access to its computers and went public with the story. Two clients, Ford and Burger King, had been charged for commercials which had never aired and they were reimbursed.

Despite the scandal at J. Walter Thompson and its former antibarter position, CBS took the plunge into barter syndication for a solid business reason. A recent Common Market survey showed a need for 500,000 hours of programming a year in Europe. That's enough programming to keep fifty-seven stations going twenty-four hours a day; since programming can easily sell for $25,000 an hour (a conservative figure), the potential European market is $12.5 billion.

The move into the international barter syndication market has put CBS in competition with the best-known of the barter syndicators, LBS Communications (formerly Lexington Broadcast Services, a division of Grey Advertising), which recently signed a joint venture to provide 545 hours of programming to Scandinavia. LBS is now invading CBS's territory by mounting the first major challenge to ABC, CBS and NBC in daytime programming. Launched in the fall of 1985, "Inday," a half-hour show featuring "soft" national news and syndicated by Tribune Broadcasting, is the linchpin of a two-hour block of first-run barter syndication programming.

With this surge in interest in barter syndication—a fully-controlled, fully commissionable situation—agencies are even more unhappy with the general run of broadcast barter. First, many local retailers don't need agencies precisely *because* barter is available to them. Take a local waterbed retailer who doesn't have money for a full schedule of radio commercials. Instead, he can offer a waterbed in exchange for an abbreviated schedule of commercials (which the station will produce for him), hold a contest and announce the winners in a remote broadcast from his store. In effect, he will have paid for the commercials with waterbeds and will have gotten away without having to pay an agency fee or commission.

On a much higher level, larger companies can do the same kind of thing through barter specialists like Media General Broadcast Services (MGBS), Broadcast Marketing and other media barterers. National manufacturers like General Electric and ITT have run campaigns involving thousands of radio and TV commercials through these firms, using excess inventory as the form of payment.

While MGBS takes pains to note in its presentation film that "Media General ad campaigns are fully commissionable to 4A agencies" (members of the American Association of Advertising Agencies), MGBS vice president Ed Hartnett understands why agencies don't get along with media barterers. He says, "One, they lose control; two, they don't get commissions in certain cases; and, three, there's a lot of uncertainty involved.

"Let's say a manufacturer is stuck with half a million felt-tip pens. He goes to a barter company, negotiates a deal he's pleased with and signs a contract to exchange them for media. Two months later—unless he's gotten great results without a single foul-up—his agency is going to tell him, 'You've been screwed,' as a matter of course.

"The solution is to make the agency part of the partnership from the outset. The barter people don't like that, but it makes for a smoother relationship. If the 4As attempted to incorporate barter in their thinking, it might be better for everyone." Unfortunately, agencies, like the clients that hire them, consider barter a dirty word and wish it would just go away. A J. Walter Thompson vice-president asks rhetorically, "Who wants to be paid in refrigerators?" And a 4A spokesperson said the organization has "no official position on barter and isn't likely to take one in the foreseeable future."

Despite this mutual antipathy, the pitched battle between barterers and agencies will not end in the foreseeable future or the year 3,000 for that matter, because the bartering of advertising time and space will never end. Simply put, the United States has far more radio and TV stations (cable and broadcast), billboards, newspapers, and magazines than advertisers will ever be able or willing to support on a cash basis.

According to *Broadcasting* magazine, the full complement of commercial, on-the-air broadcasters and cable companies currently includes 4,785 AM radio stations, 3,771 FM radio stations, 907 TV stations and 6,600 cable systems. In addition, there are also 1,688 daily newspapers, according to *Editor & Publisher,* 7,704 weekly newspapers, according to the National Newspaper Association and 11,090 periodicals, according to the *IMS Ayer Directory of Periodicals.* Leaving aside direct mail and outdoor advertising (billboards and ads on trains, buses, bus stops and shopping centers), there are 36,545 mass media outlets all fighting tooth-and-nail for the same advertising dollar.

Broadcasters are at a particular disadvantage in this battle. Owners of unsold billboards can run civic-minded public service announcements (PSAs) and promote their service with signs like "Your Message Here! Call 1-800-S-P-A-C-E-R-S." Print media are free to expand or cut back the number of pages in each issue, depending on how ad sales go. Their pages can also be traded reciprocally with other media (*Rolling Stone* and *Mother Earth News* have traded pages this way); filled with "house ads," ad copy promoting a particular section, feature or columnist; or padded with merchandising possibilities ("Preserve your treasured copies of *Smithsonian* in these handsome binders").

Unfortunately, broadcasters can't expand—or contract—the number of hours in a day. Secondly, while they can (and do) trade reciprocally with print media, they're always uneasy about helping to promote a competitive form of advertising. Finally, running the radio version of a house ad ("Your business should investigate using KZFX as an advertising medium") would be a blatant admission of how poor ad sales really are. For those reasons, broadcasters would rather barter than fill time with a commercial for a magazine or newspaper, promotional spot or PSA. Once an unsold minute of time is filled one of these ways, it's gone forever as a source of revenue, whereas bartering time for products can at least cut operating expenses.

Such bartering has to be preplanned; broadcasters can't wait until Tuesday to barter Wednesday's unsold commercials. Tom Tanski, the president of Broadcast Marketing, says, "Let's face facts; about a third of all broadcast time goes unsold. I don't know about you, but most people don't like to do things all-or-nothing. That means broadcast inventory has to be bartered *in advance.*"

What happens when it's not? Several Christmases ago, XTRA, a San Diego radio station whose transmitter is in Mexico, was given all of forty-eight hours' notice to pay $16,000 in cash bonuses to its Mexican employees or lose its license. The general manager got the $16,000 in cash, all right, but he had to sell $200,000 worth of air time to get it—better than a twelve-to-one ratio.

Naturally, a situation like this is an extreme example, but broadcasters have stoically accepted the need to preplan their bartering since the Depression, when new, cash-poor radio stations bartered with newspapers. Even though radio was competing with them for advertising dollars, newspaper advertising managers understood that the public was eager to read news about radio personalties, either in the form of ads or articles. Stations with cash bought newspaper ad space; others traded for it with scrip which they had received from the restaurants in exchange for radio advertising time.

Following radio's cue, broadcast television and cable television have bartered from their inception. Media buyers and other credible sources agree with Tanski that as much as 30 percent of all radio time (even more in small towns, less in big cities), 25 percent of all cable TV time and 20 percent of all broadcast TV time is bartered. That's tantamount to saying that America has ten radio stations for every seven, four cable channels for every three, and five TV stations for every four it can actually support through paid advertising. Because owning a TV or radio station can be so lucrative (it has often been described as "a license to print money"), entrepreneurs—too many of them—decide to build or buy stations. Given human greed and the inevitable creation of new advertising media, the glut of unsold advertising time will never vanish entirely; it will merely be bartered away.

One clue to just how established bartering is is revealed in an internal report prepared by Arthur Young & Co. for RKO General, Inc., a division of Gencorp. RKO, owner of seven radio and five TV stations in major cities, went so far as to establish standard barter rates for all its stations. RKO broadcast outlets like WOR-TV in New York traded with other stations or print media on a one-to-one basis, giving a dollar's worth of station time for a dollar's worth of newspaper space. With manufacturers of cars, carpeting and TV sets, the ratio grew to two-to-one, two dollars' worth of station time for one dollar's worth of goods. Finally, when media barterers gave stations cash, credit cards good up to a certain amount or similar charge accounts at restaurants and hotels, they got three dollars' worth of advertising time for only a dollar; in contrast, a cash customer (not you we hope) had to pay a dollar for a dollar's worth of time.

Naturally, broadcasters would prefer to sell all their time for cash; however, they are realistic enough to know that that's not always possible so they accept the need to barter and plan their bartering activities in advance. Inevitably, many firms have sprung up to exploit this unpleasant reality on behalf of their corporate clients. Media General Broadcast Services, a division of Media General, Inc. (MGI), the only *Fortune* 500 company involved in the barter business, has the financial wherewithal to leverage its buying power with both broadcasters and manufacturers.

Located in Memphis, MGBS has five interactive departments which trade goods, services and minimal amounts of cash for radio and TV time:

1. Production services—produces jingles, canned music, radio and TV commercials for broadcasters.
2. Travel trade—trades for airline tickets, hotel rooms, rental cars, cruises, etc.
3. Special products—contacts potential clients with excess inventories and also converts other goods and services into cash.
4. Media sales—converts broadcasting time into cash.
5. Media services—contacts stations and obtains air time with cash, trade or both and stores it in a "time bank," an account into which all time is "deposited" and "withdrawn" as needed.

Media Services is the fulcrum of the company and is headed by vice president and general manager Bob Stack. He says, "We sell jingles, production libraries (canned music and sound effects), station IDs and commercials for cash, trade and a combination thereof. We offer goods and services in return for air time, and we can offer anything money can buy—a car, a helicopter, a transmitter, anything. Naturally, we offer $100 worth of goods for $200 worth of time; sometimes, we can even get as high as a four-to-one ratio.

"Let's say the gm [general manager] of a radio station wants a new Volvo and wants to get it in exchange for radio time. First, we qualify the buyer. What's the station's track record? How are they doing in their marketplace? What have we done with them before? After all, that Volvo will cost me $15,000, and I'm taking the risks up front."

Supplying a Volvo in exchange for radio time is not an example plucked out of thin air. When Stack deals with stations, he goes armed with what *The Wall Street Journal* calls "a Sears, Roebuck catalog for broadcasters." Mailed around Labor Day, the catalog runs to more than 1,000 four-color, loose-leaf pages and bulges with products of every description. While companies like Apple, Xerox, RCA and Nikon don't necessarily trade with Media General, their products are listed in the catalogue cheek-by-jowl with Styrofoam beer coolers and radio station credit cards, which can be customized. Stack expains, "Stations love stuff they can slap their call letters on."

If offering stations quality merchandise at great prices doesn't work, MGBS has another ace up its sleeve, one few broadcasters would want to leave home without. American Express cards, good for purchases up to a fixed limit, are often issued to MGBS clients. While other media barterers render similar services, MGBS renders more of them; a company slide show notes, "We have the fourth or fifth largest American Express bill in the world."

As attractive as this interest-free credit option is, some general managers might still turn it down, but Stack still has one more powerful closing argument. "I'll remind him that his station has a highly volatile inventory. If it's July or January, it won't take much reminding. But if he still needs to buy a $1 million helicopter with cash, he's going to have to sell $3–4 million worth of advertising time to generate the profit to pay for it. Instead, with us involved, he gets full use from $2 million worth of time that might go unsold anyway."

Other forms of media can't be retraded as easily as broadcast time, although *Newsweek* has bartered through Atwood Richards, *Family Circle* has worked with Deerfield Communications, and the Chicago-based Pattis Group, which sells space in several hundred magazines, has a division called Tradewinds that does nothing but trade space in its clients' magazines. 3M's Media Networks, Inc., often swaps full-page ads on a regional basis in magazines like *U.S. News & World Report* and *Money,* while its billboard company, National Advertising Co., barters for furniture, computers, carpeting, and cruise tickets.

THE MEDIA-TRAVEL CONNECTION

Cruise tickets are just one element in the travel industry's vast unused inventory which is even more visible than broadcasters' unused time. While they don't realize any income from PSAs, radio and TV stations can at least fill their "dead air" with PSAs and appear to be community-minded. By contrast, airlines can't camouflage empty seats by filling them with mannequins. That's why, like broadcasters, travel firms prebarter their inventories and they do so with the very people who are most reticent about publicly revealing any connection between barter and broadcasting—advertising agencies

When an airline, a rental car company or a hotel chain interviews prospective advertising agencies, it is quickly made clear that part of the business arrangement will be denominated not in dollars but in credits; agency personnel can then use the credits for hotel rooms, rental cars, cruise accommodations, airline tickets, etc. Such allotments of credits can be considerable, however, and, since an ad agency can rarely use $100,000 worth of cruise tickets to Hawaii itself, it will find other ways to dispose of them—through travel agents, who can then turn the credits back into cash; the result is what has been termed the media-travel "gray market."

Travel agent Jim Bisciglia, owner of Cardillo Adventures in

Travel in Canoga Park, California, has been a part of this gray market for eight years. He says, "When the airline or hotel issues the credits, they know that one ad agency probably won't be able to use such large amounts, but the agency will at least be discreet about unloading it; travel-oriented ad agencies can't barter tickets openly; they have to be guarded about it, because the hotel or airline doesn't want it known that its price can be discounted through barter, and the ad agency wants to keep its client happy. In the final analysis, what happens is the ad agency discounts the credits to a travel agent like me, selling $100 worth of credits for $50 in cash. When I get the credits, I can sell them to my clients, either directly or through a trade exchange [Bisciglia belongs to three] at the regular price, and make a profit."

Lucinda Alexander of Keye/Donna/Pearlstein, a large Los Angeles ad agency, plans media expenditures for the barter portion of travel accounts like American Hawaiian Cruises (AHC). AHC spends $6–8 million annually in cash and barter, with the barter portion of the account amounting to between $1 and $2 million. She says, "We take a lot of barter and sell it for cash."

This process, known in the trade as cash conversion, is the reverse of sequential trading. Any person or firm interested in cash converting is not worried about maximizing leverage; rather, the main concern is transforming some commodity, such as travel credits, into cash. When ad agencies seek to convert credits given them by travel clients, they make such credits available cheaply to travel agents.

When the travel agent's profit margin is high enough, he may pass on part of the profit to his or her regular clients in the form of lower prices. This means that any company that does a sizable amount of traveling may be able to cut its out-of-pocket travel costs by making an arrangement with a gray-market travel agency, or, alternatively, with an ad agency that has travel accounts. The savings can be substantial for a company that flies the same route all the time, say, a manufacturing company with headquarters in Houston and a plant outside Birmingham. Working through a travel agency or ad agency, you may be able to fly more and/or pay less.

Besides working through travel agencies or ad agencies, there's a third way you may be able to conserve cash on business travel—by making a deal with a radio or TV station on which you advertise. Broadcasters often run promotional contests as bonuses for their clients, which are often travel companies. Alexander remembers a barter contest done with WXYZ-AM, the ABC affiliate in Detroit. "It wasn't the most intellectual premise—'Guess the temperature in Hawaii and win a cruise'—but it worked. People called the station to make their guesses, and we'd contact the ship's captain on the ship-to-shore radio to see how close they came. WXYZ also owns a TV station there, and they did a shot of the boat on their evening news; the contest generated a lot of extra interest." If you've already deduced that several WXYZ staffers enjoyed a Hawaiian cruise that year, you can move to the head of the class.

All this deal-making doesn't mean that there are no supply-and-demand restrictions on travel barter. As in media bartering, the second and fourth quarters are difficult times to place travel barter advertising, because print and broadcast media generally have more cash business than they can schedule. On the other hand, vacation travel business is generally light in the first quarter anyway, which is why you hear so many radio stations offering trips to Paris in off-peak months like March.

However, if you're willing to spend some time investigating, you can make an advantageous deal, particularly with hotel chains. Bill Francisco, who formerly ran the travel trade department at MGBS and is now a vice president with Ensslin & Hall, a Tampa ad agency, says, "If you're paying rack rate [full price] at a hotel, it's simply because you haven't tried to negotiate a better one."

One reason that hotels and motels barter so much is overbuilding, similar to the proliferation of radio and TV stations and cable outlets. Francisco says, "When a city gets hot—like Atlanta in the 1970s—buildings go up every other day, and, inevitably, the city becomes overbuilt with hotels and motels. It happened with Houston, and now it's happening in cities like Memphis and Knoxville, where lots of people built for the World's Fair."

Even in the absence of a building boom, hotels always get by with unfilled rooms, and owners are acutely aware of just how perishable their inventory is. At the end of 1983, there were 2.7 million hotel rooms in America, according to the American Hotel & Motel Association Educational Institute in Ann Arbor, Michigan. Yet hotels will average only 67 percent occupancy in the 1980s, according to a study done by a Los Angeles accounting firm, while other estimates have been even lower. That's like saying every hotel room in America is empty one out of every three nights, and it's a solid motivation for hotels to barter.

Francisco also points out a second motivation. "Industry statistics show that, even when people stay in a bartered room, they spend $50 a day in meals and beverages. It's safe to figure that half of that is profit, say $25. Since maintenance of a given room—salaries and supplies—amounts to $15 a day, filling an empty hotel room not only costs nothing, but it also makes the hotel a $10 cash profit. When you look at it that way, if they're trading for media, they're getting a bonus of free advertising plus a minimum $10 a day profit from bartering a room that otherwise would have been empty."

When hotels and other travel businesses barter outside the ad agency–travel agency gray market, they work through a network of people like Dave Wagenvoord, whose operation is part media, part travel and part sequential trade. His Sunshine Media is the only company with multiple offices (New York, Chicago, San Francisco, Miami, Honolulu) that specializes in making reciprocal trades for broadcast advertising and travel services and then leveraging them into cash profits.

Wagenvoord's duplex in the posh Marina City Club in Marina Del Rey, California, looks like a cross between an *Architectural Digest* photo spread and a warehouse. The downstairs houses 1,000 Norelco clean-air machines and 300 folding rubber boats; aside from a panoramic view of the Pacific Ocean, the upstairs is given over to stacks and stacks of hotel and restaurant scrip— $80,000 worth of Hilton scrip in Chicago, $40,000 worth of Sheraton scrip usable chainwide, and restaurant vouchers good at thirty restaurants in Los Angeles, twelve in Chicago and forty in New York.

Wagenvoord has been bartering for years and was part of the barter deal that saved Chrysler the first time, in 1975. The automaker's banks wouldn't lend more money based on unsold vehicles, but they did agree to lend against an inventory of prepaid advertising time. Chrysler worked through a New York company called Media Stock Exchange, which swapped the cars and trucks for media time through people like Wagenvoord. He got 1,150 cars, traded 960 in four weeks and took the remaining ninety as his commission. "Everybody else sent out letters with twelve-page contracts; I did business at a hotel bar in Hawaii and sold forty or fifty cars a day."

Trading is a way of life for Wagenvoord, who survived by converting cars and the like to cash while managing and then owning five different radio stations. "I survived by trading," he confesses. "Now, we buy hotel credits, cruise credits and media time like a bank and try to resell what we buy and leverage it; we try to cash out on the second transaction, and we use trade to convert to cash."

Wagenvoord can afford to be sanguine about barter because it's his whole business; Lucinda Alexander of Keye/Donna/Pearlstein, on the other hand, is ambivalent about barter as are most advertising people. She says, "The everything-is-barterable mentality wears on me and the other barter queens," a reference to the women in travel advertising who make barter deals and can then disperse perks like cruises, airline tickets and hotel rooms to friends and business associates. "It's fun, but keeping the details of fifty different deals in your mind is a big stress factor. It does something to you; you get to be like a used-car salesman—always wheeling and dealing. On the other hand, I have scrip for just about every restaurant in L.A."

SIX REMINDERS FOR MEDIA AND TRAVEL BARTERING

Your company *can* cut its advertising and travel budgets by being aware of the perishability of inventory in these fields and planning accordingly. The best way to do it will depend on your industry, your budget, the barterability of your own inventory, seasonal considerations and numerous other factors; however, careful planning will maximize your options if you keep in mind the following:

1. Do it yourself. It doesn't take much media expertise to trade for time with a local radio or TV station. Restaurateurs do it all the time, exchanging their excess inventory for advertising on a dollar-for-dollar basis. You may be able to make a simple reciprocal deal and save agency fees and headaches at the same time.

2. Ask about barter. When you interview advertising agencies or travel agencies, make it a point to ask if they barter. If you've already got agencies that you're happy with, ask them too. If you don't bring up the subject, it's a good bet that they won't either. If you've been doing business on a cash basis for a while with the same agency, you may be able to turn your status as a good client to financial advantage and stretch your travel or advertising budget through barter.

3. Remember your timing. When you do talk to your ad agency about travel, don't waste your time inquiring about free flights to Paris in June; those are already sold out on a cash basis. On the other hand, you *should* think about holding that regional sales conference in Hawaii in July or New York in November. Those are off-peak times, and, using barter, you may be able to cut a terrific deal for your company.

4. Put the schedule in your contract. If you've decided to work through a media barterer, don't leave the time your commercials air up to the stations' discretion. If the barter company says it can guarantee a block of time on network affiliates in six cities, put them to the test by making the advertising schedule part of your contract.

5. Investigate barter syndication. Even though it sounds like a marketing ploy reserved for big companies, you can modify the concept until it fits your particular needs. Remember that your local radio or TV station will probably *have* to barter some time and is probably sitting there waiting for a good offer. If you come up with a good programming idea, they'll jump at the idea of bartering for the time.

6. Keep in touch with your travel agent. No vendors are less known or less appreciated by their clients. You can turn this situation to your advantage by inviting yours to lunch once in a while and establishing a relationship that goes beyond the telephone. Once he or she becomes something more than just the source of an inexpensive fare or a last-minute reservation, you may get the call when a cruise line or airline unloads a limited inventory through the gray market.

Now that you've earned your wings in travel barter, it's time to meet the real high flyers of the barter world, the companies and countries that constantly deal in the cashless form of commerce—countertrade.

CHAPTER 9

COUNTERTRADE: INTERNATIONAL BARTER

Countertrade is not an economic issue; it's a political issue in the country making the countertrade demand.
—DAVE SCOTT, Lockheed Corp.

In the fifteenth century, a handful of courageous explorers boldly set sail on unknown seas for unknown lands, seeking glory for themselves, new trade routes to bring back commodities from the East and new markets for the wares of the Western monarchs or merchants who had subsidized their expeditions.

Western manufacturers still covet finding new markets for their products. And, even though the world has gotten smaller in the intervening 500 years, computers and telecommunications have made modern merchants think even bigger when it comes to expanding sales in virgin territories.

The largest corporations have been able to accommodate this vision internally. Most major manufacturers (Coca-Cola, McDonnell Douglas) had already begun establishing global sales and distribution networks when the post–World War II boom for consumer products of every description swept the globe. Unfortunately, the boom ended, and this vision of global marketing got blurry during the 1970s in the wake of the "oil crisis" which dried up currency reserves around the world. Establishing international marketing divisions had become increasingly expensive just when merchants and manufacturers began to notice that potential customers couldn't buy their products because of currency shortages.

These companies reacted in two ways; the largest manufacturers of consumer items (General Electric and General Motors) and a handful of retailers (Sears and K mart) began trading companies modeled after the Japanese trading giants and began selling the wares of other companies for cash on a fee or commission basis. Other companies began looking back to the good old days when you could trade goods back and forth without money serving as a medium of exchange. The result was a huge increase in global commerce without cash—international barter, or, as it is better known, countertrade.

James I. Walsh, a senior international economist at the U.S. Department of Commerce, defines the practice as "any contractual arrangement that commits the seller to take payment in goods and services" (i.e., instead of cash). Typical deals include Canada trading freight cars for Indonesian rubber, and McDonnell Douglas Corp. bartering aircraft for Yugoslavian transmission towers. In an even more intriguing example, ABBA, the Swedish pop music group, trades its records for items like horsemeat in Eastern Europe and, through a trader, resells it in the West to overcome regulations forbidding currency from leaving Communist countries.

Given the flexibility it offers in solving problems like these, countertrade is growing even faster than its domestic equivalent. In 1976, it amounted to a mere 3 percent of all world trade; in 1983, Commerce Department officials talked about it amounting to "20–25 percent of world trade." The Commerce Department officially projects that countertrade will constitute *half of all world trade* by the year 2000.

This soaring growth can be attributed to four factors, three of which are the same that fueled the rise of domestic barter—economic conditions, technological advances and indirect trading. The fourth, the increased respectability of trading, was never necessary outside the U.S., where barter has long been a favored method. The relaxation of East-West tensions has also led to greatly increased countertrade between the superpowers and their satellites.

Economic conditions. OPEC's stranglehold on oil caused a currency shortage that began in the mid-1970s and only let up late in the decade. Just as world commerce was recovering from that blow, the international debt crisis made business people painfully aware of just how little cash there was to oil the wheels of commerce. As a consequence, they were forced to become more used to doing business without it and not only managed but mostly prospered.

Technological advances. Combining satellites and computers has made it as easy to transfer commodities as cash worldwide since the same mechanisms are used in both cases. One trader says, "You don't stand on one side of the border and shove wheat over as they hand you vats of chemicals. You take their goods, sell them, put the cash in a blocked account, and then use the cash to fund a letter of credit." Letters of credit, machinery and bananas—just like cash—can now be represented as graphic symbols on a computer screen and can be transferred anywhere instantaneously.

Indirect trading. As we have seen, credits issued by a trade exchange or corporate broker can facilitate trading by expanding the number of trading partners and the goods and services in which payment can be made. Similarly, credits issued by countries in connection with clearing agreements (see below) can facilitate trading by eliminating the need to find a trading partner immediately. In effect, such credits are backed by governments, not businesses, reducing the chance that they will become unspendable.

Relaxed East-West tensions. Detente was good for business, a fact that was overlooked in the 1970s but is noteworthy by its absence in the tense 1980s. Western companies found eager new markets for their products in Eastern Europe, and East bloc countries were able to find markets for their locally produced machinery and foodstuffs.

When countertrade became a business buzzword (after "Theory Z" but before "greenmailing"), the world's nations approached it in different ways. The U.S. pretended it didn't exist, remaining noncommittal. Meanwhile exports declined from 21 percent in 1971 to 17 percent in 1982, and America's negative balance of payments and increased dependence on foreign investment have made the country the world's largest debtor nation.

Elsewhere, the Soviet Union and its satellites, helped by vast resources of crude oil, imported valuable technology while satisfying their citizens' demands for Western merchandise like jeans. Surfeited with dollars, OPEC nations were able to trade oil for needed agricultural items and expertise. The Third World suddenly became a valued customer for European products ranging from grooming articles to surveillance aircraft.

Aware that other companies and countries were countertrading while Uncle Sam watched in distaste, American companies decided to get in on the action and began lobbying for the government's help in stimulating exports. The Reagan administration's answer was the Export Trading Company Act of 1982, which President Reagan said would create 320,000 jobs while establishing hundreds of well-funded, savvy export trading companies (ETC's).

The Act sought to expand U.S. trade by granting ETC's complete immunity from U.S. antitrust laws, except for private party lawsuits for actual damages, and by getting American banks directly involved in trading operations to provide more export financing. (The Act allowed banks to invest up to 5 percent and loan up to 10 percent of their capital to an ETC.)

Amid much fanfare, St. Louis dentists created the Universal Trading Group to build and manage health care facilities abroad, Sacramento rice growers combined to bid on foreign government contracts, and catfish farmers in Mississippi formed the U.S. Farm-Raised Fish Trading Company.

But the idea has failed so far because of dollars, specifically the strength of the U.S. dollar through the mid-1980s. Thus far, less than fifty ETC's have been formed, and none are operating at a profit. While a few members of the Iowa Export-Import Trading

Co. have sold seed corn and hogs in Korea, the Prince Manufacturing Corp. in Sioux City, Iowa, dropped out after two years.
President Roland Juncks says, "Aside from selling one order of
twenty-five pumps in South Africa, we didn't get any new business, because the strong dollar doubles the cost of our goods."
Hugh Parnell of the Mississippi fish-trading group says, "We've
had a lot of inquiries but not much business, just one order sold to
Japan."

The failure of ETC's to fulfill their promise has been even
more depressing in the light of the rapid growth of countertrade.
ETC's, the Reagan administration's answer to reversing a record
trade defecit by expanding American cash export sales, have
failed just at the time when other countries are getting badly
needed technology, keeping people employed and providing new
foreign markets on a barter basis through countertrade.

While this practice only became fully established in the
1970s, in effect, Adolf Hitler built his war machine in the 1930s
by countertrading. Forced to seek trading partners and basic materials outside of Western Europe and North America, Hitler bartered for them, taking Malayan tin and rubber from the Dutch
East Indies for German steel, diesel engines and locomotives; he
also arranged sequential deals—exchanging German aspirin for
Yugoslavian steel, trading the steel for Central American coffee,
then swapping the coffee for manganese from the Soviet Union.

After World War II, Western companies avidly sought new
international markets for their products. At the same time, East
Bloc countries needed products to complete five-year plans, but
they didn't have the cash to finance building the factories to turn
out these goods. Moreover, Western bankers were unwilling to
extend credit to financially shaky countries which were also their
ideological enemies at the height of the Cold War. In other words,
political problems prevented willing trading partners from doing
business in cash; therefore, they needed an alternative meeting
place, middlemen and a mechanism—a "where," a "who" and a
"how."

Vienna was a logical choice for "where." It had a centralized
location, halfway between East and West, and a long-standing

reputation as a place to gather intelligence of all kinds. Finally, the city already had a clutch of legal and financial intermediaries who were used to dealing with both U.S. and U.S.S.R. allies and could switch from Communist doctrine to capitalist jargon in midsentence if need be.

With "where" and "who" out of the way, all East and West needed for the twain to meet was the right "how," which was supplied by separating a barter deal into two parts. *Business Week* explains, "What paved the way for the current explosion [of countertrade] was the innovation of splitting a primitive barter deal into two separate transactions: the original sale and the 'buyback,' or 'counterpurchase,' of goods from the customer. . . . The parallel transactions are a proxy for barter because the two payment flows wholly or partly balance out."

With the basic elements in place, countertrade began to grow slowly and then spurted with the tenfold increase in oil prices and the international debt crisis. As the practice became more familiar, many governments—particularly those with centrally planned economies—began making it mandatory. Indonesia, Belgium, Bulgaria and Romania currently require 100 percent countertrade, necessitating foreign companies or countries to buy these nations' goods on a dollar-for-dollar basis. Other nations require countertrade in specific product categories; Ecuador, for instance, demands that alcoholic beverage imports be matched dollar for dollar with banana exports.

Countertrade, like domestic politics, makes for some pretty strange bedfellows. The People's Republic of China, the world's most populous Communist nation, had worked out countertrade deals with, among others, Manischewitz and Pierre Cardin long before the current movement to China's current policy which blends capitalism and Communism into an economic system some have called "incentivized socialism." Manischewitz's parent, Monarch Wine Co., advises the PRC on brewing and bottling and is paid with the exclusive U.S. distributorship for Tsingtao beer; Pierre Cardin's company consults the Chinese on clothing manufacture and takes its pay in silks and cashmere rather than money.

This worldwide wheeling and dealing sounds intriguing, and

many executives, blinded by the international nature of countertrade, continue to envision it as a very mysterious business indeed; however, Bank of America's Daniel N. Cecchin, who's made countertrade deals for ten years, insists "There's nothing new about it; it involves the same banking mechanisms—trade financing, letters of credit and documentation—that have been required for years in cash deals."

In effect, countertrade amounts to reciprocal trading (like China and Manischewitz) or using a middleman broker (like ABBA). What makes it different from domestic deals is the political component. For instance, heightened East-West tensions killed a deal under which Control Data Corp. was to have shipped a $3 million computer to the Hermitage Museum in Leningrad; in exchange, the museum would have loaned some of its treasures for a U.S. tour and given the computer company the exclusive right to market exhibition catalogs and the like. The deal collapsed when the Soviet Union invaded Afghanistan; the U.S. government took reprisals by refusing to grant the Russians freedom from seizure, the Soviets refused to ship the art and Control Data never shipped the computer.

Despite political disruptions, countertrade can:

1. Provide scarce goods and services. During the 1973 oil crisis, Japanese businesses initially panicked about their vulnerability to oil shortages, but the government was able to recover by trading excess machinery for vast amounts of Russian crude oil. Eliot Janeway wrote in the *Atlantic Monthly* that as a result, "Japan has wound up sitting on large supplies of reserve oil at no cash cost, for which it is paying on the installment plan with industrial exports that couldn't be sold anywhere else, certainly not for cash."

2. Mandate foreign investment. Despite the current slump in oil prices, some OPEC members can use their black gold as a bargaining chip to lure Western investors. A $3.95 billion Saudi Arabian contract for the AWACS aircraft surveillance system requires successful bidders to invest $1 billion in specific kinds of ventures in Saudi Arabia.

3. Import needed technology. Even industrialized nations like Canada use countertrade to attract high technology. The Canadian government "buys" airplanes from companies like Lockheed and, in return, the aerospace giant brings industry to previously rural areas like British Columbia to fulfill their countertrade obligations.

Using countries rather than companies as trading partners has its down side of course. In addition to some familiar complaints associated with domestic barter—unusable merchandise, overused executive time spent in negotiations—the political nature of countertrade adds a few new unpleasant wrinkles:

- **Costly penalties.** Nearly all countertrade agreements involve nonperformance clauses which may include penalties of up to 50 percent of the contract. Failure to deliver can make this a very expensive way to do business.
- **Conflicting bureaucracies.** A Russian trading organization was interested in importing steel welding electrodes and insisted that its supplier take cast iron tubes or steel pipes. The Western company preferred to take back bicycles or farm machinery, but those products were the export responsibility of a different trading organization, and the trade could not be completed.
- **Concealed protectionism.** A *Wall Street Journal* editorial by Susan Lee pointed out that barter "becomes bad politics as well as bad economics when it's used to underline the mistakes of the nonmarket economies of the Comecon countries. . . . Their own creaky economies don't throw off enough imports to earn the hard currency through regular trading mechanisms, so they force their goods on the outside world through countertrade practices." Unfortunately, as Mohammad Mahathir, the prime minister of Malaysia, told the *Journal of Commerce,* "The choice is not between free trade and countertrade. It's between countertrade and no trade."

Countries like Malaysia might not have a choice about whether or not to countertrade, but there are many forms of it used to structure deals and solve problems. The seven main categories of countertrade are barter, swap, counterpurchase, compensation, blocked currency barter, clearing agreements, and switches.

BARTER

Like its domestic counterpart, international barter merely involves exchanging one commodity or product for another without the use of cash. Occidental Petroleum has made the biggest barter deal to date—a $20 billion, twenty-year arrangement under which the company agreed to ship superphosphoric acid to the Soviet Union for ammonia, urea and potash.

SWAP

In swaps, "where" is more important than "what." Essentially an offshoot of barter, swappers exchange similar products in different locations to save transportation costs, which can be considerable for commodities like petroleum. For example, in 1978, the Soviet Union supplied oil to Mexico's customers in Greece, Eastern Europe and Turkey and, similarly, Mexico supplied oil to Cuba.

COUNTERPURCHASE

As discussed in connection with aerospace, counterpurchase (also known as offset) agreements involve parallel transactions. "You buy my airplanes, and I'll help you sell your transmission towers." In 1979, General Motors sold Yugoslavia $12 million worth of locomotive and diesel engines; Yugoslavia insisted that GM buy $4 million worth of its cutting tools. GM found a Detroit manufacturer willing to take the tools and made the deal.

COMPENSATION

Under a compensation agreement (also known as buy-back or co-production), a company sells machinery, technology or both to a country and receives a large part of the factory output as its compensation. Levi Strauss wanted to expand its European operations in 1978; Hungary wanted a blue jeans plant, but couldn't pay for it in hard currency. Instead, Hungary bought equipment and experience and Levi got 60 percent of the plant's annual output. In a coproduction agreement, a mainstay of aerospace countertrade, Eastern labor usually assembles Western components, although some deals involve products manufactured and marketed by both parties.

BLOCKED CURRENCIES

Blocked currency barter (also known as local currency barter) requires a firm to sell its product for local currency, then buy specified local products with that money and export the products for later sale. For example, PepsiCo built a syrup plant in Hungary, but, because of blocked currencies, wasn't allowed to take Hungarian forints out of the country. Instead, Pepsi received as its payment for the plant half ownership of a movie produced in Hungary called *The Ninth Configuration,* written by William Peter Blatty, author of *The Exorcist.* When the movie is shown in theaters or on videocassettes around the world, Pepsi is able to get back cash on its investment.

CLEARING AGREEMENT

A clearing agreement uses "book money" to represent trade between two countries. For a specific period of time and up to a specific limit, each agrees to accept as payment for its exports a credit in a special account maintained in the other's central bank or a foreign trade bank. Debits to the clearing account of one country then pay for imports from the other. (The clearing currency need not even be the currency of either country; the French use *numéraire,* an abstract currency, to keep track.) Since clearing agreements rarely cancel out, a "swing" limits the degree to which accounts may be out of balance. If such an imbalance exists on the expiration date, the deficit may be wiped clean by the acceptance of unwanted goods or hard currency or carried over to a new agreement.

SWITCH

Clearing agreements have led logically to switch trades which resemble sequential barter deals. The switch trader (or switch house) disposes of goods on the world market that a country has agreed to accept but for which it has no use. *The Wharton Magazine* gives this real-world example: "Russia has agreed to trade its pharmaceuticals for Indian tea, but the chemicals aren't ready. It accepts the tea, contacts a switch house in Lausanne [Switzerland] which finds a German pharmaceutical company with excess inventory.

"The German company ships the goods in neutral packing for which the Russians pay the trader in hard currency at a discount from the invoice amount. The trader then subtracts his fees and pays the Germans. The cargo documents pass through Russia on the way to India. Here they are marked to indicate Russian origin and shipment for Hamburg. When the chemicals arrive in India, the switch is complete."

IN-HOUSE DEPARTMENTS

Several of these countertrade techniques are endemic to certain industries. Swaps generally involve transfers of raw materials like oil; switches often consist of foodstuffs and consumer goods; compensation is a mainstay of manufacturing countertrade. In military and aerospace circles, offsets (counterpurchases) are the accepted method of countertrade. The term stems from the fact that making a commitment to sell the buyer's goods "offsets" the cost of the military hardware on its balance of payments ledger. When a country like Portugal buys expensive airplanes from a company like Lockheed, it makes economic sense for Portugal to try to "offset" the effect the costly purchase has on its balance of payments by selling some of its own goods with the help of the seller.

Rather than use switch traders or consultants to satisfy these requirements, aerospace companies prefer to meet their offset commitments in-house, and, by and large, they have been very successful at it. One of the keys to this success is motivation. As opposed to packaged goods, aircraft are expensive to develop, build, and maintain and have a very limited market—no more than a few hundred potential customers worldwide. That gives aerospace companies lots of incentive to fulfill offset contracts.

Given the scope of such transactions (a small deal is $10 million for a single aircraft), military offsets are beyond the scope of 99 percent of all businesses; however, they are noteworthy because of the way aerospace companies used them to fuel the growth of foreign markets. Whether they deal in cash or countertrade, American multinationals have mainly taken three routes to international expansion: (1) using outside consultants, like those in Vienna; (2) forming or becoming clients of trading companies (see below); and (3) starting in-house countertrade units. Of all three possibilities, the third option has been the most consistently successful, because such units do not:

- **create administrative headaches.** They are under headquarters' control from the outset, making them responsive to top management.
- **cost a lot of money.** For the most part, in-house units are inexpensive because they involve tagging onto offices already built and staffed from previous cash business.
- **present new marketing situations.** Despite their size, aerospace companies have a knack for doing business in the real world. This can be overdone, as in the bribery scandals of the mid-1970s, when Northrop was forced to disclose that it had spent at least half a million dollars to bribe officials in Indonesia, Saudi Arabia and Iran. However, builders of surveillance aircraft and missiles deal with military intelligence, dissident generals and national security concerns all the time. Dealing in this shadowy world for years has given them insight into the trading mentality that most consumer-minded corporations lack.

By this time, the aerospace industry has nearly a twenty-year history in countertrade, which has allowed it to work out the bugs currently confronting other would-be countertrading corporations. In that span of time, such companies have learned that they can meet their offset obligations by:

1. **buying goods for their own use.** McDonnell Douglas buys a large amount of pinfeed computer paper directly from Yugoslavia as the result of an ongoing deal for DC-9s and DC-10s. In a

sense then, the company is using surplus airplanes to lower purchasing costs and open new markets at the same time.

2. selling the country's goods or services abroad. As a result of offset deals, Lockheed Corp. is promoting Canadian tourism and demonstrating Australian antigraffiti sprays in the U.S. The company routinely tries to sell its clients' products at trade shows, through direct mail and to its own suppliers where applicable.

3. subletting a manufacturing or assembling function to a client country. For example, a Northrop deal with Switzerland included a provision under which the Swiss assembled the horizontal stabilizer section of certain airframe parts, thereby saving the company labor costs and speeding up production.

That 1976 deal put countertrade in the spotlight. Switzerland bought seventy-two Northrop F-5E aircraft, but not all of the $500 million purchase price was to be paid in cash. Instead, final details committed Northrop Corp. to market $135 million worth of Swiss products—nearly 30 percent of the $500 million contract—within eight years; similarly, General Electric, which manufactures the F-5E's twin engines, made a commitment to sell $17 million worth of Swiss goods. One year later, a *Wall Street Journal* story reported that "the two companies *claim* [italics mine] to have found customers for $18 million worth of Swiss goods." The *Journal* had good reason to be skeptical, because the actual total was closer to $1 million. Moreover, the deal nearly had serious political repercussions for the U.S. government and potential economic consequences for the U.S. taxpayer. Had it not been completed, the American taxpayer would have been partially liable for liquidated damages, because the Pentagon had helped negotiate the deal.

Everett Keech, then Assistant Secretary of the Air Force (now chairman of the board of Barter Exchange [see Chapter 5]) discovered the potential liability after receiving several polite but insistent calls from the Swiss ambassador. After several high-level meetings, GE and Northrop agreed to fulfill their obligations in four more years to avoid damaging relations with the Swiss and sticking taxpayers with the bill.

The story had a happy ending for both parties. Northrop far

exceeded its original commitment of $135 million and, in fact, produced Swiss export sales of $209 million three years ahead of schedule. By 1982, *Business Week* was referring to Northrop as "the aircraft industry's No. 1 countertrader."

In fulfilling its offset obligations to the Swiss, Northrop has increased the number of Swiss companies in Saudi Arabia from twenty-five to 200, helped Holderbank win a $70 million contract for an Indonesian cement plant and gotten the Swiss involved with a $1.2 billion railroad modernization program in Paraguay. Northrop was also successful brokering Swiss products like coaxial cable, generators, refrigerators, elevators and radio transmitters to countries outside the United States. This success led to a 1981 extension of the original deal calling for thirty-eight new F-5E aircraft and spare parts worth $160 million—half cash, half credited to offset.

While Northrop contends that its way of meeting its offset commitments is proprietary, it's clear that the company draws on many tools to fulfill its obligations. These include an ever-thickening "Yellow Pages" of Swiss goods suitable for export, a huge library cataloguing materials made by Swiss manufacturers, computerized databases of Swiss goods and a statistical technique that creates potential matches of buyers and sellers.

All these factors pale beside Northrop's global presence. The in-house trading unit now has fifty-some employees tending exclusively to the needs of Switzerland, Korea and Spain, all of whom are Northrop offset clients. Northrop employees in eighty other countries contribute as well; when a Cairo employee noticed a new construction site, he helped Northrop sell a number of Swiss-made elevators. A spokesman asks rhetorically, "How many nations are represented in eighty other countries?"

As for GE, the experience of selling Swiss products proved so intriguing that the corporation eventually decided to start its own trading company. By 1982, GE Trading Co. (GETC) was formed as a wholly owned subsidiary and had a staff of 200 employees including sixty bilingual engineers in thirty countries. Yet staff and commitment weren't enough to create sales. In August 1984,

Newsweek's international edition reported that GETC had failed to sign up a single new client and was cutting its staff back drastically; however, GE has since improved its countertrade operation and claims that $1.4 billion worth of GE's $3.25 billion exports in 1984 depended on countertrade and barter.

Although GE had its problems initially, aerospace specialists have been formidable countertraders from the beginning because of their technological bent, worldwide presence and private intelligence networks. In 1968, McDonnell Douglas sold seven DC-9 jets to Yugoslavia after outbidding British Aircraft Corporation, which had presented a one-shot countertrade offer; McDonnell Douglas promised their continuing best efforts to promote Yugoslavian exports. Both sides were satisfied; Yugoslavia had established its own worldwide markets through McDonnell Douglas which had, by 1984, sold 25 DC-9's and 2 DC-10's to Yugoslavia.

At first, McDonnell Douglas earned offset credits mainly by buying products for internal company use—ashtrays, wastebaskets, etc. When the range of Yugoslavian products began to multiply, the company decided to market many of them outside as well. That's when aerospace executives began selling transmission towers, holding buyer showings to promote glassware, and—finding there was a shortage of oilfield pipe—getting Yugoslav companies to produce it.

McDonnell Douglas's arrangement with Yugoslavia has been successful in three main areas:

1. Direct purchase. Yugoslavia makes certain products for direct purchase by McDonnell Douglas—"everything from paper clips to coveralls," says Henry Orenstein, who manages the program.

2. Export development. Orenstein and other offset managers help the Yugoslavs export to certain divisions of McDonnell Douglas's supplier companies like General Electric. "Since we do business with GE's engine division, we can make direct suggestions to them, but getting their consumer products divisions involved is another story."

3. Travel. A full-time travel expert and two professionals from Kompas, the Yugoslav-owned travel company, work out of McDonnell Douglas; they recently arranged an incentive trip to Yugoslavia for 2,000 Westinghouse employees. "We use their generators in our aircraft, so we were able to make a presentation to the consumer division, and they bought the idea."

Under the Yugoslav arrangement, Douglas has also bought huge amounts of canned ham, which it had to sell in employee parking lots and cafeterias. "Some people think that's all the Yugoslavs export, but they build power plants, dredgers, truck components and aerospace tooling too. We help them market jewelry, mineral water, textiles, cookies, pretzels, sardines, jam, and beer."

Working with the Yugoslavs has created problems occasionally. Orenstein had a large shipment of wine impounded by the California Department of Weights and Measures. It seems the Yugoslavian manufacturer had used 750ml mineral water bottles, which closed with a cap; instead, after the bottles were filled with wine, a cork was inserted, leaving no way for the bottle to hold 750ml. "We were able to avoid civil and criminal penalties by explaining the situation, but the wine couldn't be sold; we had to give it away through charitable organizations."

Problems also arise from Yugoslavia's political divisions; there are six republics—Serbia, Croatia, Slovenia, Bosnia-Herzegovina, Montenegro and Macedonia—and two autonomous republics—Vojvodina and Kosovo. Each has its own foreign trade organization, and each maintains its own banking and foreign exchange accounts. Inexadria, the charter airline, is located in Ljubljana (Slovenia) and JAT, the state-owned airline, is located in Belgrade (Serbia); naturally, each stresses exports from its home republic.

Despite the problems, another manager, David McCaughey, says there are many pluses in having an offset department in-house. "We save the corporation money, generate a large amount of useful information and create business for other divisions like solar energy and information services. We could generate substantial commissions steering business to U.S. and foreign companies. More and more, I think international companies like McDonnell Douglas will become *de facto* trading company operations."

TRADING COMPANIES

While aerospace companies have taken care of countertrade commitments in-house, consumer goods manufacturers and retailers have chosen to set up trading companies that sell a wide variety of their own and other manufacturers' products all over the world. The results have been mixed with few successes (K mart), several near-disasters (GE and Sears) and several total disasters (Control Data Corp. and Massey-Ferguson).

Such operations have proven expensive to establish and difficult to administer. Most significantly, consumer-oriented American corporations seem unprepared to adopt the trading mentality (which is foreign to American corporate thinking) or to hire and give responsibility to individualistic traders. As *Fortune*'s John W. Dizard has noted, albeit overstating the case for effect, "The particular mentality of a countertrader [combines] the avarice and opportunism of a commodities trader, the inventiveness and political sensitivity of a crooked bureaucrat, and the technical knowledge of a machine tool salesman."

Aerospace companies, which are in-bred by nature, chose to forgo the potential profits of a trading company in the interests of running a tight ship. Retailers like Sears, Roebuck & Co. are in low unit-profit businesses and therefore need volume to meet sales goals. By using some of their employees' time to sell items manufactured by other companies (and charging large fees for it) they can defray the cost of those foreign offices, increase profits and help other companies market their goods worldwide.

The term "trading company" doesn't mean that such businesses are solely barter operations. Instead, they are mostly cash businesses that sell other American companies' products internationally and are equipped to deal with countertrade if necessary.

They were inspired by Mitsui and other *sogo shosha* (trading companies) which have learned how to trade over the course of more than one hundred years; some Western attempts to duplicate their success failed in matters of months. Control Data Corp. and Massey-Ferguson both folded their countertrade operations after suffering seven-figure losses; however, companies like General Motors have done well in the trading business. By now, the company has parlayed countertrading into a $100 million-plus business in nearly thirty countries and has twenty full-time employees in the U.S., Great Britain, Austria and Yugoslavia, selling ball bearings, strawberries, zinc, aluminum and fish.

Several companies noted GM's success with much interest. Sears, Roebuck & Co., which already exports to thirty countries and buys from more than 12,000 suppliers, decided to start a trading company after commissioning three separate studies—by Business International, McKinsey & Co. and Booz, Allen, & Hamilton. The consensus idea was to license Sears products in Japan, South America and Australia and to establish regional trading offices in Japan, Hong Kong, Singapore, Brazil and Mexico.

Sears invested $100 million in its trading company, and Sears World Trade (SWT) president Roderick Hills, former chairman of the Securities & Exchange Commission, predicted $5–10 billion worth of sales within five years. Instead, SWT lost $16.3 million on revenues of $120 million in fifteen months, Hills resigned, and Richard Jones, Sears' vice chairman, took over.

Some faulted the choice of Hills, despite his connections to the Reagan administration, because he lacked a trader's instinct, background or connections. Trader Roger Davis, head of New York's Countertrade Roundtable, says of Hills, "He may have been piped into the White House, but he didn't know the chief in the village."

Others faulted internal Sears politics. The SWT transactions committee had to give written approval of all deals, even when they involved major corporations. Timing, a major factor in trading, took second place to credit checks. Also, Sears's well-known and highly regarded international buying operation, which imports over $1 billion of merchandise every year, remained totally separate from the trading company.

While some observers have speculated that the buyers didn't want to tie themselves to a venture many looked on as ill-conceived, one offset manager says, "Take a situation where textiles are offset-creditable to a company like Northrop. [Meaning that they can be used to reduce an offset commitment.] Sears or K mart can help them satisfy part of their offset requirement and make a profit at the same time. That's the real reason why Sears World Trade is separate from Sears, Roebuck. J. C. Penney could conceivably buy from Sears World Trade, but it would never buy from Sears, Roebuck."

Nevertheless, while SWT remains separate from Sears, Roebuck, its countertrade unit works directly with the Sears, Roebuck buyers, and is having greater success. Phil Rowberg, vice president/countertrade, says, "We're fully integrated with the purchasing people. We've been able to take the limited trading volume of SWT and mate it with the tremendous buying power of Sears, Roebuck & Co."

The countertrade unit was established in the spring of 1984 under Rowberg, a veteran of General Motors' successful Motors Trading Company. While Rowberg is closed-mouthed about his clients, he's helped Lockheed fulfill some of its offset obligations and worked on deals with traders like Deerfield Communications. So far, he says, SWT countertrade has sold telephone systems, commercial airliners, TV sets, venetian blinds, wooden doors and barite, a mineral used in oil exploration.

Sears's largest competitor in domestic retailing—K mart Corp.—is also a competitor in foreign trading. Where Sears has run into problems, K mart's trading arm, K mart Trading Services (KTS), has prospered. KTS is run by Gerald Issler, a K mart Corp. employee for thirty-one years, who says, "We've stayed within our limits—that is, buying and selling consumable consumer-type merchandise. We haven't hired 1,600 people and then cut 10 percent of them, and we're not buying a lot of firms or creating joint ventures. We've kept it very narrow, very tight. We're working with what we already had."

K mart already had buying offices scattered throughout the Far East—Hong Kong, Seoul, Manila, Shanghai, Singapore, Taipei and Kobe, Osaka and Tokyo—as well as agents in London, Milan and Barcelona. Issler says he and seven employees in Troy, Michigan, work with 15,000 U.S. suppliers and deal mostly in cash, "although we have done barter and countertrade deals." He says, "We're selling K mart-branded merchandise in Taiwan and into Japan, but we're also selling German products in England. In 1983, we probably added five to six hundred different new products. We don't sign agreements with manufacturers; we merely ask if they want us to sell their products overseas; a lot of them do."

THINGS TO REMEMBER

If your company is large enough to consider marketing its goods and services overseas, you'll probably weigh all the pluses and minuses before going ahead with expansion that may be costly and time-consuming. However carefully you plan, though, you might want to remember the following:

1. Barter makes doing business overseas even more difficult. Specific business problems which would be minor on your home turf become major due to the strange environment and the unfamiliar method of payment. Once you've decided to go ahead with a countertrade program, allow plenty of time for bridge-building before expecting concrete results. Countertraders have to worry about currency fluctuations, terrorism, national politics, American security concerns, government bureaucracy, propaganda, local politics, cultural differences and other factors, all in the context of a business deal with foreigners. Given these circumstances, even the most well thought out plan will take time to implement.

2. Let traders manage the trading. Make sure your mechanism is run by traders, not bureaucrats, whether you hire outside firms, work through consultants or bankers, or establish branch offices. Timing, flexibility and the ability to move quickly are essential in all forms of barter and only become more important when substantial geographic distances and time changes are involved. Committees, as Sears sadly discovered, can't move quickly enough to meet the deadlines imposed by foreign barter deals. Have your administrative people set up flexible systems and then run things more loosely than normal for six months while the trading operation sorts itself out.

3. Don't be overwhelmed by the scope. When you trade that raccoon coat for your neighbor's pool cover, you're going through the same steps Saudi Arabia took when it traded $1 billion worth of crude oil for ten Boeing 747s; the only difference is the scope of the deal; the principles governing bartering remain the same. Countertrade can be confusing, particularly with its lingo and its aura of mystery. Nevertheless, business is business, even when it's being done in another country, possibly in a different language and without cash.

4. Study the credentials of "experts." Even though it's been around in one form or another for a while, countertrade as a $600 billion business is nearly brand new, so new that there is only a handful of truly experienced experts. Many countertraders pass themselves off as authorities on the basis of only a handful of deals. As Dave McCaughey of McDonnell Douglas put it, "Once countertrade got a lot of ink, all the James Bond guys came out of the woodwork." Check references, call business friends in common, question the Commerce or State Department about a given company or trader.

5. Use your powerful friends in Washington. Even though Uncle Sam has dragged his heels on countertrade, the U.S. Commerce Department has unparalleled resources to help businesses thinking of expanding abroad. In addition to a clutch of qualified experts on trade financing, health restrictions, agricultural conditions, tariffs and dozen of other topics, Commerce has more than 140 "country" experts—one each for nearly every nation in the world. If you manufacture catcher's mitts, the experts on Bahrain, Brunei and Burundi will let you know whether or not baseball has caught on in these particular areas.

We've observed the way countertrades work, how sequential traders, corporate brokers and trade exchanges operate, and the ways broadcasters, banks, governments and multinationals swap excess inventories back and forth in the present. It's time to examine the specifics of how all these disparate elements will exchange goods and services in the future.

CHAPTER 10

THE FUTURE
OF BARTER

People tend to forget everything they learned about bartering in their childhood; the scope is so much larger than they're used to dealing with that they get flustered.
—DENNIS NEEDHAM, *Commonwealth Trading Corp.*

Despite this difference in scale, despite its intricacies, despite the negative publicity surrounding it, despite the unscrupulous individuals that are often attracted to it, despite a marked absence of regulations governing it, barter has a very bright, almost limitless future. It is able to overcome such negatives, because barter is flexible, versatile and inevitable.

Flexibility. Barter is, in certain cases, preferable to cash as a medium of commerce, because it can often make transactions possible that can't be concluded in hard currency.

1. As we have seen, one section of the U.S. Internal Revenue Code defers enormous tax bites indefinitely when real estate is swapped while another confers sizable deductions immediately through gifts-in-kind.

2. Due to its inherent flexibility, barter can overcome artificial political obstacles to commerce, such as blocked currencies. In one case, we've discovered how ABBA was able to trade its records for commodities in Eastern Europe, then resell them for cash; in a second deal, we've seen the way an Argentinian plantation was traded for another and paid for in a boatload of bananas, which was subsequently resold to overcome restrictions on cash leaving the country.

3. Barter is an available alternative in situations where shortages of cash impede trade. That state of affairs—the international debt crisis—is one reason for the rapid growth of countertrade. Barter can also offer a means of debt repayment when cash is not available. (Remember how Commonwealth satisfied a bad debt for CBS by bartering sporting goods for airline tickets?)

4. Barter credits are also preferable to cash where nearly unsalable inventories are involved. Receivables deals (Chapters 8 and 9) help manufacturers dispose of inventories by converting them into receivable trade credits good for advertising and other commodities.

Versatility. Barter can conserve cash, create new customers and channels of distribution, produce introductions to cash customers, boost promotional budgets, reduce payroll costs, provide incentives for dealers and distributors, and raise employee morale.

More recently, barter has also been used to:

1. Reduce competition. Times Mirror Corp. traded cable TV systems in Arkansas, New Jersey and Kentucky and $10 million in cash for Storer Broadcasting-owned systems in Arizona and California allowing both companies to enhance their presence in those states. Similarly, chain owners of newspapers have swapped morning newspapers in some markets for afternoon papers in others to create profitable near-monopoly situations.

2. Guarantee sources of supply. Computer manufacturers are dependent on semiconductor suppliers and lose sleep over the possibility of business failures, strikes, terrorism or natural disasters which would threaten their supplies. For that reason, chipmakers like Intel and Advanced Micro Devices barter their semiconductor technology with each other to guarantee their manufacturer customers of *two* sources of supply in case of an emergency. Called "second-sourcing," the technique has spread beyond the semiconductor business into other areas of computer manufacturing.

3. Comply with regulations. Forced by FCC rules to divest itself of the *Daily News* after acquiring KTLA-TV in Los Angeles, the Tribune Company, publishers of the *Chicago Tribune* and other newspapers, sought to barter this thriving newspaper rather than sell it for a relatively low amount of cash within a specified period of time.

Inevitability. We've already seen that barter is inevitable in broadcasting where, on the average, ten radio stations can only find seven cash buyers. A similar situation exists in the hotel business, which only averages 67 percent occupancy and tends to overbuild in certain "hot" cities, and, in the airline industry, where a "load factor" (a percentage of the airline's occupied seats) of 63 percent is viewed as an absolute boom period.

Such underconsumption of inventory is no less prevalent in manufacturing. No business person wants to risk losing a cash sale because an item isn't physically available for a customer to buy. The end result is pandemic overproduction that cuts across all industries, markets and distribution systems.

Over and above this general rule of thumb, specific industries overproduce when they become "hot," i.e., receive concentrated doses of consumer enthusiasm before eventually becoming yesterday's retailing news. If you want to know which ones are overproduced at which times, simply take a stroll through off-price retailers like Marshalls and Pic'n'Save. Video games? Personal computers? Michael Jackson dolls? Trivial Pursuit? They're all there currently—and at drastically reduced prices.

While these three factors—flexibility, versatility and inevitability—insure that barter will be with us now and probably forever, business conditions will continue to change, and barter will change with them. It seems likely that the future holds the following:

1. Government will increase its role in barter.

Although it took a while, the federal government is increasingly becoming involved in regulating barter, both on its own initiative and at the urging of the trade exchange industry. Nevertheless, Uncle Sam still resists trading, so several states are pursuing it on their own. While Tennessee and Iowa have formed export trading companies to help small business exports (see Chapter 9), Florida has taken a big step toward making itself a power in Caribbean trading circles.

In July 1984, the Florida legislature passed a law establishing the International Currency and Barter Exchange of the Americas. This nonprofit corporation is modeled after the Insurance Exchange of the Americas bill, created in 1979 to keep insurance business in the state. It's intended to increase the state's trade with Central and South America by concentrating on barter and countertrade. The Exchange will meet costs by (1) selling seats on the exchange to brokers, who will try to create deals, and syndicators, who will take title to goods; (2) earning transaction fees and (3) providing warehousing, telephone, telex and office services to members.

2. Banks will overcome their fear of trading.

The explosion of countertrade is causing banks to become more barter-minded for several reasons: (1) They're acting more and more as clearing houses for trading companies; (2) they're making deals by matching buyers and sellers which were outlawed before passage of the Export Trading Company Act; (3) *The Economist* reports that Kleinwort Benson, the British merchant bank, does, in fact, make barter deals on its own account through a subsidiary called Fendrake. "Fendrake arranges barter deals, and, if it cannot find a buyer immediately, holds on to goods until it can."

Perhaps most important, banks only handle an estimated one percent of all countertrade deals and would like to initiate more deals and generate more commissions. As Daniel Cecchin of Bank of America says, "It's only natural that a bank get involved in countertrade. It's just another means of financing a deal. Despite the rapid growth of countertrade, the great majority of American companies doing business overseas don't have the expertise or contacts to conclude such transactions."

And, even though no bank has as yet started a successful export trading company, such enterprises could become very successful in the future. Fred Howell, a senior international economist with the Department of Commerce, says, "Bank ETC's are sleepers; they've got the intelligence networks, the offices and the personnel; they might really do well with trading." *Fortune* goes even further, predicting, "Commodities houses and international banks will probably end up dominating the business."

3. Trade exchanges will become more respectable.

As the result of adverse media coverage, numerous consumer complaints and an industry shakeout, trade exchanges are now attracting a better grade of client. One typical satisfied customer is the University of Detroit, which offers tuition, basketball tickets and psychological counseling to earn trade dollars and spends them on office supplies, sidewalk repairs and capital equipment.

The attraction for major corporations working through trade exchanges will continue to be the tantalizing lure of new business, particularly customers they can't identify using traditional marketing techniques. Xerox never knew there was a substantial market for used copiers until the company traded them through Barter Systems. While companies like 3M and Republic Airlines have had poor results using this method, Continental Airlines's experience with Barter Systems showed that 60 percent of all the people that flew on trade were incremental passengers—completely new customers—while another 30 percent represented business taken from other airlines. Such potential will no doubt lead other major corporations to try trade exchanges again, particularly with more solid, more corporate-minded trade exchanges on the rise.

4. Corporate brokers, media and travel barterers will consolidate.

Corporate barter brokers are already undergoing a period of crisis similar to the one which bedeviled trade exchanges several years ago. Both of the new public barter companies—Univex and IBI—were having their problems satisfying corporate clients, Atwood Richards has been beset by threatened lawsuits, and Media General Broadcast Services was having trouble keeping its old customers from the William Tanner days, because Media General doesn't have Tanner's savvy in cutting deals with broadcasters; according to one insider, MGBS's business has shrunk 35 percent since his imprisonment on fraud charges.

All this presages a shake-up similar to the one already going on in the trade exchange field, most probably by merger. While corporate brokers, sequential traders and media and travel barterers have slightly different methods of operation, they tap many of the same sources—hotel chains, airlines, broadcasters, seasonal merchandisers, etc. Since there is only a finite amount of broadcast time, hotel rooms, and airline tickets available for trade, it is possible that companies who trade commodities like these will merge eventually to increase profitability.

5. Countertrade will continue to grow.

A 1983 National Foreign Trade Council survey of major corporations showed that 97 percent of the respondents surveyed expected countertrade to keep growing. One bellwether for the future may be the way McDonnell Douglas was able to license the technology of a client country, arranging a joint venture between Ikarus, a Hungarian bus manufacturer, and Crown Coach, a Los Angeles manufacturer of school buses. The final product had a Hungarian body and chassis with a Cummins diesel engine, Rockwell axles, a GM transmission and Thermo King air conditioning. The joint venture sold 243 buses, and the Ikarus share was $27 million.

On balance, barter has a bullish future; however, it won't become established as a standard technique until a few myths are exploded.

▪ **Barter is not simple.** It is not a childhood game, not a magical road to riches, not a panacea for inventory problems; it requires a different mind set and, often, different methods, than does working with cash. Moreover, it won't work in certain industries, certain countries or at certain times of the year for reasons already enumerated.

But, it *is* a flexible, versatile and creative business tool that has wide application to the businesses of professionals, small companies, large corporations and countries of every political ideology. Unfortunately, some business people become blinded by its supposed crystal-clear simplicity and overlook the numerous complexities attendant on using it correctly today. While the basic formula hasn't changed in 5,000 years, the context has; when the Indians traded Manhattan for jewelry, there were no labor unions, no federal laws, no government agencies and no tariffs.

While the business climate has changed, and keeps changing daily, people within the barter business persist in imputing magical powers to trading when they approach clients. These men and women (whose experience, I might add, lies largely outside normal business education and corporate training) tend to gloss over the complexities of what they do and reach for simplistic analogies, such as "It's like trading baseball cards" or "We're a bank, but we don't use money."

Empty phrases such as these simply will not register positively with the very clients barter businesses would most like to have. Trading baseball cards is simple, direct and cheap. It doesn't involve local politics and national security (like countertrade), operate with multiple parties involved (like media and travel bartering), or require expensive legal and tax advice (like mortgage swaps).

■ **Simple-minded selling leads to disappointed clients.** Sadly, barter companies, for the most part, prefer to keep their clients unknowledgeable and happy, the business analogue of barefoot and pregnant. Rather than point out the pitfalls, barter companies tend to gloss over the rough spots that are a part of the barter marketplace. When problems do arise, their clients suddenly and belatedly discover that they've been spoonfed only part of the truth.

One reason for this information gap is that countertraders, trade exchange owners and corporate brokers are often forced to pitch clients from a defensive position, given barter's checkered past. Hundreds of business people *have* gotten burned in barter deals, and traders have to overcome the memories of these sour deals before they can point out the benefits of their own programs. In a sense, then, every trader inherits and is forced to work with every broken promise and blue-sky offer ever uttered by another barterer.

■ **Some business people who got burned deserved it.** Many business people who badmouth barter are the same overoptimistic souls who put aside normal business sense during their first and only experience. While they have no doubt conveniently forgotten the haste with which they wanted to dump the inventory they had on hand, they haven't forgotten that, "We had a bad experience. Everybody in barter is a crook."

Because barter has been viewed as an "underground" activity (despite being a multibillion dollar business), it has attracted many unscrupulous people; however, if Jack Webb taught us anything on "Dragnet," it was that con games, scams and bunco schemes only work on already greedy victims. Similarly, overblown promises about the wonders of bartering only hook people who have set aside their natural skepticism and continue to put their trust in self-proclaimed barter miracle workers.

Bob Twersky, head of the Special Products Division at Media General Broadcast Services, says, "Many executives treat bartering the same way they would deal with buying a car; they go to four places and pick the least expensive without ever even kicking the tires."

He says Media General recently lost out on a $2 million deal because the competition offered a part-cash/part-trade media plan which would only cost the client (a computer component manufacturer) $800,000 in cash and $1.2 million in excess inventory versus Twersky's offer of $1.2 million in cash and $800,000 in inventory. Twersky says, "The manufacturer had an inventory we pegged at being worth fifteen cents on the dollar; for the other media company to come out on the deal, they would have had to have raised sixty cents on the dollar from that same inventory.

"That was clearly impossible. If the client had really thought about it, he would have realized there was no way his inventory could bring that kind of return. If he would have gotten sixty cents on the dollar, he wouldn't have been bartering in the first place. Like too many executives, this client only heard what he wanted to hear."

What the client heard was, "top 20 markets . . . sports and prime time in the fourth quarter . . . performance bond . . . arbitration in case of any misunderstanding." What he didn't want to devote much time or effort to thinking about was:

1. "How can this company barter for media in the top 20 markets at the hottest selling season of the year—Christmas?
2. How can they guarantee media placement on a barter basis on sports events (football and basketball) and prime time TV—the hottest advertising commodities?
3. What criteria would a bank (which knows nothing about media placement) use to decide whether the conditions of the performance bond are being met?
4. Why does this company keep insisting on arbitration as a method of settling disputes? Why should I rely on arbitration, which could amount to no better than a fifty-fifty proposition, rather than go through the regular legal system when I'm fulfilling my part of the agreement upfront?"

All these unasked questions stem from what Tom Tanksi calls "the ego component of barter." Tanski asks, "What manufacturer can admit that his baby is defective?" The answer is, "Not many." This inability to make such an admission coupled with the barter company's extravagant promises are virtually a formula for failure. To put it mathematically, Client's wishful thinking plus Barter company's unrealistic promises equals Disaster.

The computer component manufacturer would prefer to believe his product is worth four times what Media General is offering for it, because of his ego involvement and his failure to admit marketing or production mistakes. For its part, the barter company will promise whatever it takes to make the deal now and worry about the fulfillment end later.

What is needed is a new patch of common ground on which

barterers and business people can meet. Each side has to learn (and unlearn) a few things before barter can be used more effectively. Barterers have to:

▪ **Think long-term.** Their standard litany is "Never approach sales managers or finance people. If you don't talk to the president, you're wasting your time." That's true for barter companies who are only interested in building short-term relationships. It's very easy to sell a generalist CEO or CFO who knows nothing about the intricacies of media. Twersky says, "The bigger the company, the easier it is to snow somebody, because the larger the company, the less direct specific experience the CEO or CFO has with barter."

However, new barter companies like Commonwealth Trading and Barter Exchange are trying to establish long-term relationships with long-term clients. Instead of trying to snowball one big deal into being, they're taking the time to talk to marketing people, purchasing people, finance people, lower-level people who can receive their message, understand it, get excited about it and pass it on with a favorable recommendation to someone higher up.

▪ **Present all the facts.** Barterers can help you solve problems, but only when they show you the whole picture. Barter will become a permanent part of the business arsenal only when barterers begin to say things like "Mr. Smith, we'll be able to get you some cash and some media time for your inventory, but you're not going to get sixty cents on the dollar, and your commercials aren't going to be seen nationally on the *Today* show. I'm sure your corn popper is an excellent product, but, right now, it can't be sold for cash at the price you want; that's the reason you're talking with us. However, we may be able to get you as much as twenty-five cents on the dollar and spots on some high-ranking daytime shows in Sacramento, Savannah, Columbus, Albany and forty-six other secondary markets."

▪ **Learn how to say no.** Barter will have come of age as a business tool when a trader can look an executive straight in the eye and say, "Ms. Jones, your situation is unique, and, as much as I hate to admit it, I'm very sorry to say that we can't help you. I don't like to turn away business, but, frankly, if I were in your shoes, I'd talk with Swappco, because they're better equipped to deal with this kind of thing than we are." Such a conversation won't get an order today, but it might create a genuinely enthusiastic referral tomorrow.

For their part, business people have to learn to:

■ **Research possible vendors assiduously.** Successful barter companies either present or will supply on request lists of satisfied customers. Call these people. If the barterers were applying for jobs, you'd check their references, wouldn't you? One barterer lists a contact at a major company who didn't initiate the barter program and, frankly, wasn't very satisfied with it; I found out, because I called to check it. If you've made a connection through a business associate, question him or her carefully about the details. If you've been cold-called, ask for and check bank references, local and state business associations, industry trade associations and law enforcement officials.

■ **State demands specifically.** If you're only interested in trading to get a specific item without paying cash, say so. Don't be satisfied with a fuzzy "best efforts" clause, and don't be misled by nonspecific oral "guarantees." Remember that above-board companies will attach performance guarantees to your contracts. Even so, if you're bartering for broadcasting time, for instance, call some of the stations listed to find out if the barterer has fairly represented what the station is willing to offer.

■ **Think ahead.** When barter is discussed internally, planned and provided for in advance, it works well; however, barter is a lot riskier option when it's a last-gasp solution to moving an inventory. When it's not preplanned, low offers have to be accepted reluctantly because of time pressures. New product launches are festive occasions when enthusiasm runs high at all levels; however, *somebody* should be thinking about the down side. "What happens if this product doesn't fly? How will we get rid of it? Who should we call? How should we plan to go about that without disrupting our distribution network? How can we assure getting the maximum mileage out of it if we *are* forced to liquidate?"

When clients learn to ask tough questions like these in advance, when they investigate how finance, purchasing and marketing will react to a barter deal before the fact, and when they adopt realistic attitudes about the worth of their goods, they will eliminate much of the fear and uncertainty currently connected with bartering.

Similarly, when barter companies learn to approach companies with long-term relationships in mind from the beginning, when they learn to explain the intricacies rather than explaining them away and, most of all, when they can objectively see where they fit in—and where they don't—barter will begin to overcome its negative history and become a positive business tool for businesses of all sizes.

Of course, getting traders to think in terms that the average business person can relate to is going to be difficult, given their experience and orientation. Generally speaking, they are flamboyant, optimistic, charming people. It is not mere coincidence that Bill Tanner has 400 suits color-coordinated with 400 ties, and 800 shirts that match an equal number of ties; there's a reason that Mort Binn has *two* telephones in each of his two limousines.

Business people like Tanner and Binn were born traders. Their attitude towards doing business is much like that of the Russian peasant who had a mangy old dog and told an incredulous friend that he expected to realize 2,000 rubles from selling it. "Boris," the friend snorted, "you'll be lucky to get 200 for that mutt."

When they met a month later, the friend asked, "What happened to that dog of yours?" Boris replied, "I sold him for 2,000 rubles." The friend responded, "You must be joking." "No," the peasant shrugged, "I was fortunate enough to find a pet dealer with two cats available at 1,000 rubles apiece."

RESOURCES

This list of resources was compiled purely for informational purposes, and all listings were factually correct as of February 1, 1986; however, neither the author nor the publisher bears any responsibility for accuracy of the information beyond that date, or, for the conduct, honesty or responsiveness of any given business or publication involved in barter or countertrade.

THE BASICS

While more than five hundred national magazine and newspaper articles about barter have been indexed, someone interested in more information may find the following stories helpful:

- "All About Barter," *Wharton Magazine,* Summer 1979. A good survey piece with a useful section on countertrade as well.
- "Bartering Grows Among Big Companies," *The Wall Street Journal,* October 18, 1980. A good though dated survey of major corporations and their bartering.
- "The Great American Barter Game," *Across the Board,* January 1981. A group of related articles touching on trade exchanges, corporate bartering, etc.
- "Marketing without Money," *Harvard Business Review,* November-December 1982. Good advice on the drawbacks of barter.
- "Thriving Without Money," *Quest/80,* July-August 1980.

149

A clutch of related articles touching on many aspects of barter.

- "Trade Secrets," *Inc.*, August 1982. The single best survey piece on business bartering.

I've already mentioned the three best general books on barter—*Back to Barter* (Proulx), *The Barter Book* (Simon), and *Let's Try Barter* (Wilson). Wilson's book is full of interesting facts and challenging ideas about barter and concludes with an excellent Afterword by Karl Hess, a former speechwriter for Senator Barry Goldwater, which puts barter in a sociological perspective.

While *The Only Barter Book You'll Ever Need* (Bantam Books, New York, 1984) and *How to Barter* (Comstock Trading Company, Walnut Creek, California, 1980) devote sections to real estate exchanging, the best single book on this growing phenomenon (and its tax implications) is *A Fortune at Your Feet* (Harcourt Brace Jovanovich, New York, 1981) written by A. D. Kessler, who hosts an annual real estate exchangors' convention and also edits the leading magazine in the field—*Creative Real Estate* (Box 2446, Leucadia, CA 92024).

Naturally, all questions regarding barter and taxation should be directed not only to your accountant but also to the Internal Revenue Service. (Check your local telephone directory under U.S. Government or call 1-800-424-1040). For more technical information on barter and the IRS, see articles in the *Journal of Taxation* listed in the Bibliography.

If you want to explore gifts-in-kind, see David Johnston's story in the *Los Angeles Times* (October 26, 1984), "Corporations Are Increasing In-Kind Gifts," or contact the two national organizations which handle them:

Gifts in Kind
United Way of America
United Way Plaza
Alexandria, VA 22314
(703) 836-7100

National Association for the
Exchange of Industrial Resources
540 Frontage Road
Northfield, IL 60093
(312) 446-9111

RECIPROCAL TRADE

The three barter books mentioned above all have detailed descriptions of reciprocal trades, and *New York* magazine (January 17, 1977) ran a lengthy piece on numerous aspects of barter including reciprocal trading called "Reintroducing Barter."

Any of the generalized articles mentioned in the Bibliography ("Using Barter as a Way of Doing Business," "Back to Barter," "Firms See Bartering as Good Deal") include material about reciprocal trades. Trade magazines and daily newspapers cover business swaps as they occur. When Lufthansa swapped $3.5 million worth of aircraft parts for oil owned by Ramco International, *Aviation Week* (September 15, 1980) had the story; similarly, *Madison Avenue* (November, 1984) covered swapping merchandise for promotion in "Let's Make a Deal." When Republic Airlines and Pillsbury Corp. swapped airline tickets for land, the story was carried by the *New York Times* (March 3, 1983).

TRADE EXCHANGES

Two of the best stories on trade exchanges are: "Barter Firms Add New Twist to Old Game" (*Barron's*, November 7, 1983) and "Barter Boom Keeps on Growing" (*U.S. News & World Report*, September 21, 1981). *The Only Barter Book You'll Ever Need* (Bantam Books, New York, 1984) offers an overview of trade exchanges plus an informative chapter on how to start and run one.

As mentioned, *Barter News* is the only current periodical covering barter. The quarterly publication covers all areas of barter but places particular emphasis on trade exchanges. P.O. Box 3024, Mission Viejo, California 92690, (714) 855-4618.

The trade association for trade exchanges, the misnamed International Reciprocal Trade Association (IRTA), is also a source for information on exchanges, legislation, etc. Write to IRTA, 4012 Moss Place, Alexandria, VA 22304 or call (703) 823-8707.

CORPORATE BROKERS

Three 1981 *New York Times* stories—"Boom in Barter" (March 15), "Barter: Comic Books to Big Jets" (May 9) and "Barter Becomes Big Business" (July 26) serve as a quick guide to the corporate side of barter. *Forbes* gives a thumbnail sketch of the workings of the receivables deal in "Write-off Avoidance" (May 1, 1982). Selected corporate barterers include:

Atwood Richards
99 Park Ave.
New York, NY 10017
(212) 490-1414

Commonwealth Trading Corp.
511 11th Ave. South, #270
Minneapolis, MN 55415
(612) 332-6019

Corporate Trade Center
511 11th Ave. South, Box 80
Minneapolis, MN 55415
(612) 333-3200

Universal Trade Exchange
1 Madison Ave.
New York, NY 10010
(212) 684-7722

TRAVEL AND MEDIA

One of the earliest and best pieces on this subject is "A Barter Boom in Advertising," a story on Chrysler's bid to divest its 1975 inventory (*Business Week,* April 7, 1975). (See Chapter 9.) For a fascinating look at the former king of the media barterers see "The Sultan of Swap" (*Fortune,* July 26, 1982), a discussion of William Tanner as well as the way receivables deals are applied in media.

When Tanner's empire began to fall, there was extensive coverage in *Advertising Age* and the Southeast Edition of *Adweek* (August 15–29, 1985) as well as in *The Wall Street Journal* (August 12–29, 1985). *Advertising Age* also did extensive coverage of the Marie Luisi–J. Walter Thompson barter syndication scandal (February 8–April 26, 1982). Barter syndication has become a regular area of coverage in *Broadcasting, Television Radio Age* and *Electronic Media* as well as the show business trade papers, *Variety* and the *Hollywood Reporter.*

Media and travel barterers operate nationally, including Sunshine Media which operates under other names in different cities. The leading firms are:

Alan R. Hackel Org.
1330 Centre St.
Newton Centre, MA 02159
(617) 965-4400

Media General Broadcast Services
2714 Union Ave. Extended
Memphis, TN 38112
(901) 320-4212

Broadcast Marketing
551 5th Ave.
New York, NY 10176
(212) 370-1777

Sunshine Media
4316 Marina City Drive #333
Marina Del Rey, CA 90291
(213) 823-2069

COUNTERTRADE

Amid the avalanche of clippings on countertrade, no single source has been as consistently lucid and entertaining as John W. Dizard of *Fortune,* whose story, "The Explosion of International Barter" (February 7, 1983), amounts to a primer on the field. Other periodicals noteworthy for their continuing coverage include *The Wall Street Journal,* which covered the subject early ("U.S. Firms Pressed to Offer Barter" [May 18, 1977]), *Countertrade Outlook* and *Business International,* the weekly newsletter for multinational corporations (see below).

The export trading company concept has been explained in depth by *Inc.* and *The Wall Street Journal.* The small business magazine ran a good story about export trading companies when they showed promise ("Trading Places," November 1983); the *Journal* explained why they have yet to fulfill it ("Export-Trading Firms Are Failing," May 24, 1984).

Four publications track countertrade on a weekly and quarterly basis. The weeklies are:

Business International
1 Dag Hammarskjold Plaza
New York, NY 10017
(212) 750-6300

Countertrade Outlook
P.O. Box 3141
Alexandria, VA 22302
(703) 370-3817

The quarterlies are:

Countertrade & Barter Int'l
World Trade Center #316
Boston, MA 02210
(617) 542-7833

Countertrade & Barter
Quarterly
708 3rd Ave.
New York, NY 10017
(212) 490-0791

Several entrepreneurs have echoed Phil Rowberg's comment that "the only people getting rich on countertrade are those giving seminars or writing about it." One enterprising graduate student named Steven Graubart is charging $1,250 for his master's thesis on the subject (*The World of Countertrade,* Business Trend Analysts, May 1983) while *Eastern Europe: New Ways to Sell, Finance and Countertrade* is available at $1,425 from Business International Corp. The parsimonious among us can probably get by with the same company's budget-priced *Threats and Opportunities of Global Countertrade* at $385.

Moving another step down the financial scale, Manufacturers Hanover Trust Co. has created looseleaf countertrade manuals for both the Pacific Rim and Latin America which sell for $295 apiece. They can be ordered by writing John Carlson at 270 Park Ave., New York, NY 10017, or calling (212) 286-3171. Similarly, *The Economist* has published a book called *North/South Countertrade* which is available for $200 at 10 Rockefeller Plaza, New York, NY 10020, (212) 541-5730.

The two best books in the field are also the two lowest in price. *Countertrade, Barter & Offset* (McGraw-Hill, 1984, $24.95) was written by Pompiliu Verzariu, who has served with the International Trade Association in Washington for ten years; *Trade Without Money* (Law and Business, Inc., 1984, $50.00) is authored by Leo Welt, an active countertrader also based in Washington.

BIBLIOGRAPHY

ARTICLES

"Airlines Barter Air Travel." *Business Week,* July 7, 1980, p. 20.

"All About Barter." *Wharton Magazine,* Summer 1979, p. 60.

"Another JWT Money Flap." *Advertising Age,* February 8, 1982, p. 1.

"Back to Barter." *The Banker,* January 1983, p. 12.

"Back to Barter?" *Forbes,* March 12, 1984, p. 40.

"The 'Barter' Alternative." *Los Angeles Magazine,* September 1977, p. 118.

"Barter and Taxes." *Trader's Journal,* June-July 1982, p. 8.

"Barter As Protectionism." *Wall Street Journal,* October 25, 1982, p. 26.

"Barter: Banks Move In." *The Economist,* February 4, 1984, p. 83.

"Barter Baron." *New Yorker,* September 20, 1976, p. 33.

"Barter Becomes Big Business." *New York Times,* July 26, 1981, sec. 3, p. 15.

"Barter Boom." *Louisville Courier-Journal,* March 4, 1984, sec. E, p. 6.

"A Barter Boom in Advertising." *Business Week,* April 7, 1975, p. 52.

"Barter Boom Keeps Growing." *U.S. News & World Report,* September 21, 1981, p. 55.

"Barter Brokers for Big Business." *Venture,* April 1984, p. 126.

"Barter Can Mean Business." *Real Estate Today,* April 1982, p. 43.

"Barter Clubs, 'John Doe' Summonses." *Journal of Taxation,* June 1982, p. 368.

"Barter: Comic Books to Big Jets." *New York Times,* May 9, 1981, p. 19.

"Barter Company Trades in Complaints." *Our Town,* October 30, 1983, p. 1.

155

"Barter Deals Spread." *U.S. News & World Report,* January 16, 1984.

"Barter Firm Injunction." *Daily News of Los Angeles,* October 2, 1984, sec. 4, p. 3.

"Barter Firms Add New Twist to Old Game." *Barron's,* November 7, 1983, p. 42.

"Barter Gets Exporting Back in Balance." *Florida Trend,* July 1983, p. 99.

"Barter Growing Portion of Trade." *New York Times,* August 15, 1983, p. 21.

"Barter Growth." *Television/Radio Age,* December 19, 1983, p. 41.

"Barter May Create Phantom Values." *Best's Review,* July 1982, p. 58.

"Barter No Longer Thought Tacky." *Los Angeles Times,* May 22, 1977, p. 1.

"Barter Pays the Rent for California Firm." *Cashflow,* September 1984, p. 46.

"Barter Standing Grows." *Television/Radio Age,* October 10, 1983, p. 33.

"Barter, the Latest Thing." *New York Times,* May 6, 1973, sec. 3, p. 3.

"Barter: Today's Market Sweetener." *Real Estate Today,* April 1982, p. 38.

"Barter Trade." *The Economist,* February 20, 1982, p. 78.

"Barter TV Heads Overseas." *Electronic Media,* October 20, 1983, p. 17.

"Barter with East Urged." *New York Times,* December 30, 1982, p. 31.

"Barterers Beware." *Forbes,* August 17, 1981, p. 102.

"Bartering Aids Poor Nations." *New York Times,* January 17, 1983, p. 21.

"Bartering Gets New Lease on Life." *Journal of Commerce,* February 7, 1979, p. 1.

"Bartering Grows Among Big Companies." *Wall Street Journal,* October 18, 1980, p. 1.

"Barters and Buy-backs." *Business Horizons,* June 1980, p. 54.

"Blair Downgrades Barter Yield." *Broadcasting,* December 5, 1983, p. 52.

"The Boom in Barter." *Electronic Media,* January 31, 1985, p. 1.

"Boom in Barter." *New York Times,* March 15, 1981, sec. 3, p. F15.

"Boomlet in Bartering." *Dun's Review,* November 1976, p. 36.

"Burger King Swap." *New York Times,* March 3, 1983, sec. 2, p. 31.

"CB Quarter Review." *Countertrade & Barter Quarterly,* Autumn 1984, p. 8.

"Campbell, Others Probe Dealings." *Advertising Age,* August 22, 1983, p. 1.

"Chrysler Ignores Deal." *Dayton (Oh.) News,* February 3, 1980, Dorfman, p. 27.

"Controller Confirms He Was Source." *Wall Street Journal,* August 18, 1983, p. 2.

"Coproduction Boosts Arms Sales." *Wall Street Journal,* July 12, 1984, p. 40.

"Corporate Barter." *New York Times,* February 20, 1983, sec. 3, p. F4.

"Corporations Increase In-Kind Gifts." *Los Angeles Times,* October 26, 1984, sec. 5, p. 1.

"Countertrade: A Modernized Barter System." *OECD Observer,* January 1982, p. 12.

"Countertrade Phenomenon." *Business International,* December 23, 1983, p. 1.

"Countertrading Grows." *Wall Street Journal,* March 13, 1985, p. 1.

"Court Cases Offer Insights." *Wall Street Journal,* August 29, 1983, p. 1.

"Debacle in World Trade." *Newsweek* (International), August 20, 1984, p. 39.

"Economics & Politics of Countertrade." *The World Economy,* June 1983, p. 159.

"Eiffel Tower Restaurant." *New York Times,* January 18, 1983, p. 42.

"Exchanging." *Eton Journal of Real Estate,* July-August 1981, p. 12.

"The Explosion of International Barter." *Fortune,* February 7, 1983, p. 88.

"Export Trading Companies." *Business America,* March 19, 1984, p. 3.

"Export-Trading Firms Are Failing." *Wall Street Journal,* May 24, 1984, p. 1.

"FBI Impounds Tanner Records." *Broadcasting,* August 22, 1983, p. 27.

"FCC Orders Review." *Los Angeles Times,* November 10, 1984, sec. 5, p. 1.

"A Fair Exchange." *Financial World,* September 5, 1984, p. 34.

"Federal Reserve Glossary," Federal Reserve System, May 1981.

"Final Regs Affect Barter." *Standard Federal Tax Reports*, December 30, 1983, p. 1.

"Final Regulations Issued by IRS." *Journal of Taxation*, June 1983, p. 376.

"Firms See Bartering as Good Deal." *Los Angeles Times*, June 8, 1982, p. 1.

"Foreign Trade: Barter." *U.S. News & World Report*, December 3, 1979, p. 95.

"Former Tanner Exec Talks." *Adweek* (Southeast Edition), August 29, 1983, p. 1.

"GE Bets on Healthy World Trade Growth." *Industry Week*, July 12, 1982, p. 27.

"Global Countertrade Motown Style." *Business Marketing*, January 1984, p. 55.

"The Godmother." *Time*, April 12, 1982, p. 65.

"The Great American Barter Game." *Across the Board*, January 1981, p. 11.

"The Great Complacent Debtor." *Los Angeles Times*, October 5, 1984, sec. 2, p. 5.

"The House That Tanner Built." *Newsweek*, August 29, 1983, p. 55.

"IRS Clarifies Order." *Journal of Taxation*, September 1983, p. 181.

"In the Shadows of Madison Ave." *New York Times*, February 28, 1982, sec. 3, p. F1.

"JWT Striving to Overcome Luisi Scandal." *Advertising Age*, April 26, 1982, p. 1.

"JWT Will Quit Time Banking." *Advertising Age*, March 8, 1982, p. 1.

"JWT Writeoff $30 Million." *Advertising Age*, April 5, 1982, p. 1.

"LBS 'Answers' Barter Questions." *Television/Radio Age*, December 19, 1983, p. 43.

"LBS Opens Daytime Challenge to Webs." *Variety*, July 18, 1984, p. 105.

"Let's Make a Deal." *Madison Avenue*, November 1984, p. 54.

"Little Switzerland Thinks Big." *Defense & Foreign Affairs*, December 1982, p. 12.

"MGM/UA Building Barter Film Web." *Variety* weekly, July 25, 1984, p. 1.

"Marketing without Money." *Harvard Business Review*, November-December 1982, p. 72.

"A Meeting Ground for Corporate Barterers." *Business Week*, March 19, 1984, p. 47.

"Miami Bankers." *Euromoney Trade Finance Report,* May 1984, p. 31.

"Modern Barter." *Time,* June 11, 1984, p. 48.

"More Wind in Yankee Traders' Sails." *Nation's Business,* January 1983, p. 62.

"New Restrictions on World Trade." *Business Week,* July 19, 1982, p.118.

"New Rules Affect Property Swaps." *Los Angeles Times,* February 14, 1985, sec. 4, p. 3.

"New Saudi Twist." *Business International,* May 11, 1984, p. 1.

"New Tool for American Business." *Business America,* October 18, 1982, p. 3.

"Oil Prices Hit the Skids." *Business Week,* August 13, 1984, p. 54.

"Profiting From Countertrade." *Harvard Business Review,* May-June 1984, p. 8.

"A Race to Collect East Bloc Debt." *Business Week,* March 22, 1982, p. 86.

"Raking in a Bundle in the Barter Business." *Business Week,* September 3, 1979, p. 104.

"Rebuttal on Blair Barter Report." *Television/Radio Age,* December 19, 1983, p. 88.

"Reintroducing Barter." *New York,* January 17, 1977, p. 27.

"Republic Air Barters." *New York Times,* March 3, 1983, sec. 2, p. 31.

"Sears' Humbled Trading Empire." *Fortune,* June 25, 1984, p. 71.

"Selling It at the Movies." *Newsweek,* July 4, 1983, p. 46.

"Showing Products in Movies." *Hollywood Reporter,* June 8, 1984, p. 1.

"Sixth Circuit Bars Shortcut." *Journal of Taxation,* July 1983, p. 58.

"Stamps As Currency." *New York Times,* November 11, 1984, sec. 2, p. 34.

"The Strange Case of Marie Luisi." *New York,* March 8, 1982, p. 14.

"The Sultan of Swap." *Fortune,* July 26, 1982, p. 80.

"Swapathon." *Time,* November 9, 1981, p. 74.

"Swapping Property to Defer Taxes." *New York Times,* January 20, 1985, p. F11.

"The Swap Shop." *Toronto Star,* July 12, 1979, sec. 1, p. 1.

"Syndicators Sticking with Barter." *Advertising Age,* January 9, 1984, p. 45.

"Tanner: Pushing Barter to Limit." *Advertising Age,* August 22, 1983, p.1.

"Tax Equity & Fiscal Responsibility Act." U.S. Government Printing Office, August 17, 1982.

"Thriving Without Money." *Quest/80,* July-August 1980, p. 43.

"Times Mirror, Storer Swap." *Los Angeles Times,* June 30, 1984, sec. 4, p. 1.

"Time to Barter." *Atlantic Monthly,* March 1979, p. 118.

"Trade Offsets in Military Sales." General Accounting Office, April 13, 1984.

"Traders Rediscover Barter." *Los Angeles Times,* March 12, 1984, sec. 4, p. 2.

"Trade Secrets." *Inc.,* August 1982, p. 69.

"Trading Game." *Newsweek,* August 1, 1977, p. 62.

"Trading Places." *Inc.,* November 1983, p. 139.

"Trend of Second-Sourcing." *San Francisco Chronicle,* December 26, 1983, p. 57.

"Tribune Co. Hopes to Trade." *Los Angeles Times,* July 9, 1985, sec. 4, p. 1.

"Turn in Your Hats and Balloons." *Forbes,* July 2, 1984, p. 44.

"Uncle Sam May Trade Farm Products." *Transactions,* June-July 1983, p. 4.

"U.S. Currency." Federal Reserve Board, June 1980.

"U.S. Firms Pressed to Offer Barter." *Wall Street Journal,* May 18, 1977, p. 1.

"U.S. Latins Find Swapping Rewarding." *Miami Herald,* April 25, 1983, p. 62.

"U.S. May Ease Countertrade Stance." *Journal of Commerce,* Sept. 7, 1983, p. 1.

"U.S. Probing Tanner Taxes." *Advertising Age,* August 15, 1983, p. 1.

"Using Barter As a Way of Doing Business." *Business Week,* August 4, 1980, p. 57.

"WB Jumps Into Ad-Hoc Fray." *Variety* (weekly), August 8, 1984, p. 43.

"Why the Big Apple Shines." *Business Week,* July 23, 1984, p. 100.

"A Worry for Washington." *Los Angeles Times,* June 5, 1983, sec. 2, p. 1.

"Write-off Avoidance." *Forbes,* May 1, 1982, p. 56.

BOOKS

Angell, Norman. *The Story of Money.* Frederick A. Stokes Co., 1929.

Bogart, E. L. and D. L. Kemmerer. *Economic History of the American People.* Longmans, Green & Co., 1930.

Ederer, Rupert J. *The Evolution of Money*. Public Affairs Press, 1964.

Einzig, Paul. *Primitive Money*. Eyre and Spottiswoode, 1949.

Hepburn, A. Barton. *A History of Currency in the United States*. Augustus M. Kelley, 1967.

Herskovits, M. J. *Economic Anthropology*. Alfred A. Knopf, 1952.

London, David W. *How to Barter*. Comstock Trading Company, 1980.

Matison, Jim, and Russ Mack. *The Only Barter Book You'll Ever Need*. Bantam Books, 1984.

Proulx, Annie. *Back to Barter*. Pocket Books, 1981.

Schlesinger, Arthur M., Jr. *The Almanac of American History*. G. P. Putnam's Sons, 1983.

Seuling, Barbara. *You Can't Count a Billion Dollars*. Doubleday & Co., 1979.

Simon, Dyanne Asimow. *The Barter Book*. E. P. Dutton, 1979.

Smith, Adam. *The Money Game*. Vintage Books, 1976.

————. *Paper Money*. Dell, 1981.

"The Story of Money." *Bulletin of the Buffalo Society of Natural Sciences*, 1936.

Toffler, Alvin. *The Third Wave*. Bantam Books, 1981.

Tuccile, Jerome. *Inside the Underground Economy*. Signet Books, 1982.

Verzariu, Pompiliu. *Countertrade, Barter and Offset*. McGraw-Hill, 1984.

Wechsberg, Joseph. *The Merchant Bankers*. Pocket Books, 1975.

Wilson, Charles Morrow. *Let's Try Barter*. Devin-Adair, 1976.